The search fo
Bones into the pat

A shipwreck c　　　　　　 ᴏꜰ ɪᴛᴀʟʏ sends Maddock and Bones on the hunt for the legendary tomb of Alaric I and his long-lost treasure. With dangers all around, a spy in their midst, and an old enemy lurking in the shadows, can they stay alive long enough to unlock the secret of THE TOMB?

Praise for The Dane Maddock Adventures!

"A great read that provides lots of action, and thoughtful insight as well, into strange realms that are sometimes best left unexplored." *Paul Kemprecos, author of Cool Blue Tomb*

"Dane and Bones.... Together they're unstoppable. Rip-roaring action from start to finish. Wit and humor throughout. Just one question - how soon until the next one? Because I can't wait." *Graham Brown, author of Shadows of the Midnight Sun*

"David Wood has done it again. Quest takes you on an expedition that leads down a trail of adventure and thrills!" *David L. Golemon, Author of the Event Group series*

"A non-stop thrill ride triple threat- smart, funny and mysterious!" *Jeremy Robinson, author of Instinct and Threshold*

THE TOMB

A DANE MADDOCK ADVENTURE

DAVID WOOD
RICK CHESLER

THE TOMB

Published by Adrenaline Press
www.adrenaline.press

Adrenaline Press is an imprint of Gryphonwood Press
www.gryphonwoodpress.com

Cover design by Kent Holloway

Edited by Sean Ellis and Melissa Bowersock

ISBN-13: 978-1-940095-88-2
ISBN-10: 1-940095-88-3

BOOKS and SERIES by DAVID WOOD

Outpost
Arcanum
Magus
Brainwash
Herald
Maug

Jade Ihara Adventures (with Sean Ellis)
Oracle
Changeling
Exile

Bones Bonebrake Adventures
Primitive
The Book of Bones
Skin and Bones
Venom

Jake Crowley Adventures (with Alan Baxter)
Blood Codex
Anubis Key

Brock Stone Adventures
Arena of Souls
Track of the Beast (forthcoming)

Myrmidon Files (with Sean Ellis)
Destiny
Mystic

Sam Aston Investigations (with Alan Baxter)
Primordial
Overlord

BOOKS by RICK CHESLER

PROLOGUE

Cosentia, Italy 410 C.E.

Ataulf took a last glance at his brother-in-law's body before it would be interred. The fever had come quickly and left even more so, leaving the dead body of a forty-year-old leader in its wake. Suddenly Alaric the Visigoth was no more. The broad-chested, powerfully built man, with his wild mane of dark hair and shaggy beard, had struck fear into the hearts of his enemies on the field of battle. But now, death had diminished him. Gone was his fierce scowl, replaced with a calm serenity.

"You will be missed, brother." With a flick of his finger he ordered his men to close the lid on the hastily carved stone casket. A man of Alaric's stature deserved better, but it was not to be. The lid slid into place with a dull *thunk*, and the men began lowering it into the tomb.

In accordance with tradition, Alaric's body was laid to rest in a north-south alignment. All around him lay the customary sacrificial meats: goat, mutton, poultry, and pork, along with cooked eggs. Offerings of drink were laid above his head, along with mugs, bowls, and other vessels. There was, of course, much more within the tomb, and it fell to Ataulf to ensure that no one ever found it.

"I wish I did not have to do this," he whispered. But he knew what had to be done.

Although the funeral rites had ended, many people still lingered, most of them stunned in the aftermath of their leader's passing but eager to please Ataulf, as he took the reins of power.

His thoughts were interrupted by a squat, waddling man approaching. Gento was one of his best supervisors for all things non-military. Concern marred his craggy face. He nodded in the direction of the closed casket as he spoke.

"That last piece does not belong in the tomb, Ataulf. Let us have it."

Ataulf glared menacingly. "You have plenty of treasure already, Gento."

Gento hesitated but still had argument left in him. "But the most valuable…"

"That belongs to God and will *not* be destroyed!" Ataulf's face was red with anger. He expected his subordinate to turn and go at this point but, unbelievably, the man pressed on in even more assertive fashion.

"It is not my wish alone, Ataulf! Some of the men are threatening to dig up the grave if this goes with it." Gento turned to gaze down at the casket while Ataulf's hand went to the hilt of the sword sheathed on his waist. "And I am inclined to support them. With all respect, I simply cannot stand idly by while…"

He let out a grunt as his sentence was interrupted by the blade of Ataulf's sword jabbing through his gut and very nearly penetrating through his back. He turned his head to look at his slayer, realizing now that he had made a fatal mistake in averting his gaze in the first place. But he had been lost in impassioned thought as he spoke his last words, far too lost.

Disbelief flooded his eyes, quickly turning to fear as he watched his life's blood flow from his body. His lips worked, but only a bloody froth oozed from the corners of his mouth. With a wet, ragged breath, he slumped to the ground.

Athaulf shook his head. The man was the first, but he would not be the last.

The grinding of stone on stone was like comforting music to Ataulf's ears as the tomb was sealed and covered over with earth and rock. He smiled while he gazed down at Alaric's final resting place. Finally, it was done. His reverie was interrupted by the footfalls of a man running and he turned around. One of his warriors, a tall man drenched in sweat, came to stop in front of him.

"Ataulf…" He took a moment to catch his breath before being able to deliver his message. "All of the laborers have been killed. Their bodies were disposed of in the river." It was clear from the distasteful expression on the soldier's face that he was less than supportive of this action, but had carried it out nonetheless. Ataulf placed his hand on the soldier's shoulder, a comforting gesture.

"The secret must be protected at all costs. You know this. You have done well." Now Ataulf reached his other arm around the man as if to hug him. He pulled him closer in a heartfelt embrace, and then the soldier was saying how he understood, how it had to be done, how there was no other way. "I understand it, but that doesn't mean I like it, Ataulf. But at the same time, I know trust is a weakness for us now."

A dagger now protruded from Ataulf's left sleeve. Its metal glinted once in the light as he drove it through his warrior's heart.

"You are right," he said." I am truly sorry, and I thank you for your service, but even you cannot be trusted."

CHAPTER 1

The Strait of Messina

Dane Maddock grinned behind his scuba mask as the ocean bottom came into view. There was something about that moment when the seafloor first became visible after dropping down through the water that never got old, like a hidden world opening its gates for him to enter. A few feet off to his right, a big man of Native American ancestry—Uriah "Bones" Bonebrake—also made his descent. A former U.S. Navy SEAL who had served with Maddock, Bones became a partner in the treasure hunting outfit Maddock had started after leaving the Navy. The two had grown accustomed in recent years to travelling around the world on relatively short notice in search of sunken treasure and fabled historical artifacts.

A flurry of cloudy water caught Maddock's attention. He pointed down and to his left, where the other two members of their underwater team, Willis Sanders and Matt Barnaby, were already at work. Willis, tall and dark-skinned, was also an ex-SEAL who served with Maddock and Bones during their early Navy days. Matt was not a former SEAL, but was ex-military, having served as an Army Ranger, a fact that was the source of unending ribbing on the part of the rest of the team.

Maddock tapped Bones on the shoulder and signaled off to their right, to a patch of seafloor they had dove earlier. That spot had yielded some minor artifacts—a few bits and pieces of old weaponry like spears, daggers, and swords, which they had examined on board the ship and guessed them likely to be from the fifth century. Maddock thought it worth spending one more dive on the same area, which they had previously laid out with a measured grid called a transect. He and Bones reached the transect and began carefully sifting through the seabed, fanning away the silt with their hands.

Willis and Matt handled the heavy equipment—a vacuum suction device connected to the ship that removed large quantities of mud from the bottom at the expense of ruining underwater visibility. They would dredge up the sediments out of the way and then return on a later dive once the water had cleared. But Maddock and Bones had already been through that process on this site and so now were able to sift through what had been revealed.

Maddock frowned as he held up another worn slab of metal, most likely a fragment from a dagger or sword. He dropped it into a mesh bag clipped to his waist. It would aid in their identification of the wreck site, but by itself it was certainly no treasure. In addition to the literal pressure of the seawater pushing down on him, Maddock also felt the never-ending pressure the sole proprietor of an inherently risky business was subjected to. As the owner of a small treasure salvage company, he knew he had to come up with goods that he was able to legally sell for profit, or else find some other line of work. While this site was promising, it had so far failed to turn up anything that could really pay the bills.

He looked over at Bones in time to see the Indian let a shard of useless metal drop back to the seabed. Maddock was about to suggest to his dive buddy that they move to a different part of the transect when he heard the rap-tap-tap of metal on metal coming from some distance away. Most of the seabed was mud and rock, so the only way to produce that kind of sound was either from the ship itself, or from the divers. And since it wasn't him or Bones…

Maddock kicked off the bottom toward Willis and Matt while motioning for Bones to follow. The pair of divers swam over the ocean bottom until they passed out of their designated search area. They continued toward Willis and Matt. To Maddock, the metallic clanking noise had sounded like a crude signal of some kind, perhaps one of them banging a dive knife against his metal air tank, which was a common way to signal underwater.

Another noise grew louder as they drew nearer to Willis and Matt, that of the suction machinery they were using to pull mud from the bottom. A metal tube called an elbow extended up to the ship. The other end plowed into the bottom in order to suck up the sediments in order for the divers to see what was buried beneath. The suction of the machine made a loud racket, sort of a whining hum that seemed to come from everywhere at once. But piercing through the hum came that metallic clinking again.

Maddock pushed forward and then he saw the situation. And it was a situation; that much was for sure. Willis' sizable back was to Maddock, while Matt was nowhere to be seen. Willis stood with his feet planted on the bottom while reaching up with his hands. Maddock followed his outstretched arms, and when the turbulent water cleared for a moment, he got a view of what was happening.

Predicament, he thought. Matt was in a real pickle

right about now. Somehow the diver had been sucked up the intake end of the elbow tube, so much so that only his fins protruded from the end of the pipe. And yet the pipe suction was still on. They had no way to communicate to their team member on the boat, Corey Dean. Unlike the rest of the team, Corey had no military background at all, but his technical systems expertise meant that he was more than useful in a support role when it came to operating ships, computers and equipment of various kinds while the rest of the team was in the field. Still, the underwater team had no direct voice communications link to Corey topside on the boat. The suction pipe was turned on at the beginning of the dive and off at the end of it. Maddock's independent operation could not afford state-of-the-art equipment, just the meat-and-potatoes basics that would get them up and running.

And now Corey was up and running, all right, Maddock thought, watching as the beefy Willis struggled to pull his dive buddy out of the tube by his legs. About to be run up through the tube...to the ship's propeller where it connected. The force of the prop running in reverse provided the upward water suction to clear the seabed. But now it threatened to make mincemeat out of Matt unless they could either get him out of there or somehow tell Corey to shut off the engine.

Maddock tapped Bones on the shoulder and pointed up at the silhouetted hull of their boat, the *Sea Foam*, while mouthing the words, *shut it off!* Bones, seeing the urgency of the circumstances, wasted no time with a reply but instead immediately shot toward the surface. Fortunately they were in shallow enough water that the bends would not be an issue with this dive, even after a relatively rapid ascent. With Bones on the way to Corey on the boat, Maddock swam the remaining distance to Willis and the trapped Matt.

As Maddock swam up to the intake pipe, he could see that Willis was straining to keep Matt from being sucked up the elbow, so-called because it bent sharply in order to connect to the boat's propeller, like an upside-down "L." Maddock looked through Willis' mask to see eyes wide as saucers, an expression that said he was about to lose his grip on the wayward Matt.

Maddock looked up into the tube and saw that Willis only had one hand on one of Matt's fins. And then while he watched, that fin came off in Willis' hand. He heard a muffled cry of dismay carry from behind his breathing mouthpiece through the water. Matt immediately splayed his arms and legs out against the sides of the pipe to slow his ascent, but the power of the suction was too much. He was dragged up the pipe toward the boat's propeller.

Maddock wasted no time, acting on the instincts that had served him well time and time again during his time as a SEAL and as a treasure hunter. He signaled for Willis to move out of the way and then pushed off the bottom hard with both feet, shooting straight up into the tube. As soon as he was inside of it he felt the rush of water begin to carry him rapidly upwards.

He didn't think Bones would take much longer to reach Corey on the boat, but at the same time he knew Matt might only have a few seconds. He was counting on the near ninety-degree bend near the top of the elbow to stop Matt from being sucked directly into the prop, but what if it didn't? He shoved aside thoughts of blood-red water drifting down on him after the engines were shut off a little too late.

Not wanting to give that scenario a chance to unfold, Maddock reached up toward the single swim fin he saw sticking down into the vertical portion of the shaft. Most of Matt's body was already in the horizontal portion of the pipe that connected to the motor's prop. With a final, powerful kick of his fins, Maddock pushed himself up and clasped a hand around Matt's ankle, not wanting to take a chance that the fin would pull off like the other one.

Maddock wedged his own feet against the sides of the pipe as he yanked down on Matt's leg. As soon as he could he grabbed a hold of his other leg as well, and then redoubled his efforts to get him out of the dangerous horizontal section of pipe. It worked, and looking up he could see Matt's bone white face looking down on him, eyes wide, jaws clenched hard around his scuba regulator.

A second after that, the rumbling thunder of the boat's engine came to a halt and silence settled over them. Bones had reached Corey. The upward surge of the water ceased immediately. Maddock released his grip on Matt's lower legs and both divers eased their way down and out of the pipe, where Willis still stood on the bottom looking up.

Willis flashed Maddock and Matt the okay sign—forefinger and thumb held in a circle—and both men immediately responded with an okay sign of their own. Willis exhaled a long stream of bubbles in relief. But Maddock was looking at Matt, or at Matt's hands to be specific. He hadn't noticed it in the elbow, but Matt clutched a small box. Not a piece of dive gear, but something that looked old—it looked like an artifact.

Maddock pointed to it and then looked into Matt's eyes. In return, Matt turned and pointed a little behind them near one of the "blow holes" created by the elbow that they had been working. Excited now, Maddock jerked a thumb toward the surface, signaling that they should get to the boat. He knew Matt wouldn't be foolish enough to try and open the box while still underwater. If it was watertight, they wouldn't want to flood the contents.

After a slow and cautious ascent during which the trio of divers met Bones, who had jumped back in after the boat motor was shut down to see if his friends might need help, all four divers climbed onto the boat's dive platform. After quickly removing their gear, they huddled with Corey on deck. The redhead was already on the marine radio preparing to alert other boaters in the area in case they should require serious medical assistance, but once he saw everyone was okay he put down the transmitter.

"What's that?" Corey gestured to the metal box in Matt's hand.

"Haven't opened it yet, but it's heavy," Matt said as he placed the find onto the work surface they used for sorting through finds. "I think the box itself must be made of lead."

"Let's have a look." Maddock picked it up and turned it over in his hands. He could make out a thin seam where the top and bottom halves joined, but there was no latch or lock of any kind. He pulled gently on the top lid but it didn't budge.

Bones let out an impatient huff of breath and stepped up next to Maddock. "Maybe you should let me have a try."

Maddock glared at him and refocused his attention on the box. As a professional marine salvor, he knew that applying excessive force to any item that could be potential treasure was a no-no. But he tried again, applying slow but deliberate force, and after a few seconds was rewarded with a *pop* as the two halves separated. Maddock wanted to turn his head away with the onslaught of strong musty odor that wafted out of the box, but the contents were too alluring. The others caught sight of glimmering metal and crowded around for a closer look.

"Hell, yes. I see some coinage. All is gold that glitters!" Bones leaned in enthusiastically, eyes sparkling with excitement.

Maddock squinted at the coins. "They look Roman to me." He picked one up and eyeballed it closely. "Fifth-century! It's worn, but still readable."

"What's the other stuff?" Willis flipped his hand in a "hurry up" gesture as he eyed the rest of the box's contents.

Maddock picked up a small dagger with a hilt made of gold and passed it to Willis, and then carefully took out a jewel-encrusted, ornately engraved cross and gave it over to Matt for closer inspection. Then his hands returned to the container and he removed a hunk of gold shaped like an insect, with two blue gemstones for eyes that twinkled in the sunlight.

"Is that what I think it is?" Bones wanted to know.

"It's a scarab." Maddock turned the rare object over in his hands.

"Man, this is some good stuff," Willis marveled as his eyes took in the artifacts. The sheer amount of the haul wasn't impressive, but the quality and obvious value of the pieces was undeniable. They had stumbled onto something big.

"What are those two pieces right there?" Corey pointed into the box at two flat metal sculptures, each shaped like a falcon, so thin as to give them a two-dimensional appearance. Each had a large hole in the center in addition to being perforated with several smaller holes.

"What's the matter, Maddock—you don't look happy." Maddock nodded slowly. He knew his friend could read him well enough by now to know that something was distracting him from the elation he should have felt at finding such a unique hoard.

"You know, it's odd."

"What's odd, you? We know that. Surely you're not contemplating that now." Bones grinned down at his friend and business partner. Maddock ignored him and continued.

"The falcon is a pagan artifact—Visigoth—while the cross is a Christian one." Maddock turned one of the falcons over slowly in his hands while Bones took the other. At length, Bones asked, "Does the name Flavius Honorius Augustus mean anything to you?"

Maddock shrugged. " I don't know, why?"

"Because we've got the dude's dagger."

Maddock's heart raced and his hands felt numb. He couldn't believe what he was looking at. If he was correct...

"I can't be certain, but I think I know whose treasure we've found."

Bones looked up from the falcon. "Don't keep us in suspense, bro."

Maddock hesitated, then grinned. "I'm pretty sure

this belonged to Alaric, the Visigoth who sacked Rome."

CHAPTER 2

Cosenza, Italy

The Alaric Museum sat atop a small hill in the midst of Consenza, a city nestled in a lush, green valley between the Sila plateau and the coastal mountains of southwestern Italy. Formerly called Cosentia, the town was reputed to be the burial site of Alaric.

Maddock pulled their rented Renault into a marked stall in the parking lot and he and Bones exited the vehicle. They had left Matt, Willis, and Corey on the boat to continue diving the artifact site in the hopes of finding more treasure, as well as to safeguard the site from the curious who may have observed their activity. In the meantime, Maddock was hoping he and Bones might be able to shed some light on the history of the relics they had recovered so far with a little professional help from a local expert. This approach had proven worthwhile on occasion, and so he figured it was worth the relatively short trip from the dive site to the museum. Diving for treasure was seventy-five percent research, twenty-five percent hard work, and ten percent luck, he'd heard it said, reminding him they needed to give the proverbial one hundred ten percent to be successful on this outing.

He could tell by the number of cars in the lot that the place was not crowded at the moment, a small miracle they were grateful for. The building was a sprawling one-story affair with white stucco walls and well-manicured gardens. Maddock and Bones walked along a path of paver stones bordered by freshly cut grass until they reached the main entrance, which was little more than a front door propped all the way open. Inside they could see ceiling fans spinning and hear a couple of people engaged in casual conversation.

"Cosenza," Bones said. "You know what that makes me think of?"

"Of course I do. He always wanted to visit here."

Marco Cosenza, nicknamed "Coach," was an old friend of Maddock's father, and had also been Maddock's little league baseball coach. What was more, he was the original owner of Maddock's boat, *Sea Foam.*

"We'll raise a glass to him later," Bones said as they approached the entrance.

They passed through the doorway. There was no one taking money for admission, but a clay amphora stood on a table next to a sign in multiple languages reading, DONATIONS WELCOME.

"You got the admission covered, boss?" Bones asked, not breaking his stride as he passed the sign. Maddock stopped, fished a few bills out of his pocket and dropped them into the old-looking jar, which he guessed was probably a replica. This main room was larger than they would have guessed by looking at the outside. Many interesting artifacts were on display around the room, including ancient boats reconstructed from their original, salvaged timbers, multiple rows of earthen pots and many more amphora and cooking utensils. Complementing these mostly wood and clay items was an array of metal weapons including swords, daggers, shields, and crude armor.

Maddock and Bones had stopped in front of a glass case containing an assortment of spears when they were approached by an attractive woman with big brown eyes and long, glossy, black hair which she wore in a ponytail. She smiled warmly and extended an arm, shaking hands first with Bones, who had somehow seen her coming and positioned himself accordingly, and then Maddock.

"Hello, I am Adelina Franco, Director of the Alaric Museum," she said in accented English. "Call me Lina, please."

"Hi Lina, call me Bones. Or, you can just call me."

Maddock rolled his eyes while the tall Cherokee flashed his most winning smile.

"And your friend here?" Lina asked, turning toward Maddock.

"Dane Maddock, very pleased to meet you. Looks like a wonderfully interesting museum you have here."

A sad smile flitted across Lina's face. "Thank you. Not everyone feels that way."

"Why not?" Maddock asked.

"A museum dedicated to a man who sacked Rome is viewed as heresy by many. Some went so far as to compare it to a museum devoted to Hitler." She made a face. "That's a bit extreme."

"Alaric is tied firmly to Cosenza's history," Maddock said. "I don't see how he could be ignored."

Lina nodded. "Thankfully, most people agree with you." She waved an arm around at the room's artifacts and treasures. "Feel free to walk around for as long as you like and really enjoy yourself. I just wanted to let you know I was here in case you had any questions." She checked her wristwatch. "We do have a docent who conducts general tours, but I'm afraid the next one doesn't begin for almost an hour."

Bones feigned a sad expression. "Well, I guess we'll just have to spend a little quality time with you, then. My understanding of the period is pretty thorough, you see, but I'm sure if you and I got together we could, you know, fill each other's gaps."

Maddock cleared his throat loudly and gave Bones a long, level look. "What my friend here is trying to say," he said, making eye contact with the museum director, "is that we do in fact have some specific questions we were hoping an expert such as yourself might be able to shed some light on."

Lina raised an eyebrow and glanced at Bones, clearly wondering where this was going. Maddock pulled one of the flat metal falcons from his jacket pocket while nodding to Bones, who produced the dagger, holding it by the end of the blade and offering it to Lina, golden handle first. Maddock couldn't help but smile a little as her mouth dropped open upon holding first the dagger, and then a little more after Maddock handed her the falcon. She inspected the items, turning them over in her hands, brow furrowed, before tearing her gaze away from the recovered artifacts to look at Maddock and Bones.

"Where did you get these?" She quickly looked around at the rest of the museum, whether to make sure no one else required assistance, or to make sure no one was observing them, Maddock wasn't sure. He nodded at the artifacts.

"We were on a dive, in international waters." Maddock made sure to add that important, detail before continuing, lest she accuse them of pillaging national treasures. The truth was, they'd been skirting the edge of international waters. He believed his team was in the clear, but she might not feel the same way. "We found these items along with a few coins. We were wondering if they could possibly be from Alaric's lost fleet?"

There it was, he thought, his hopes and dreams laid out on the table to either be dashed or to have something made from them. He didn't have long to wait in order to find out. Lina slowly tore her gaze from the finds.

"I believe so." Her voice carried a dazed, bewildered tone. "In fact, I'm almost certain of it. I'm not sure how much you know about the history of it, but when Alaric and his Visigoths sacked Rome, they not only raided the public buildings, but private homes of the wealthy, too. A dagger that belonged to the Roman Emperor of the day would have been a great prize for Alaric, and legends hold that he helped himself to some of Flavius's belongings in order to shame him."

"Spoils of war," Bones said, admiring the artifacts in a new light.

Lina nodded. "What else did you find besides these and coins?"

Bones looked to Maddock, who hesitated before looking at Lina. "We also found a jeweled cross and a gold scarab."

Lina's eyes seemed to sparkle with intensity. "Wow," she said in a hushed voice, almost to herself before lapsing off into thought.

"Wow what?" Bones prompted.

Lina snapped out of it. "Now I'm even more convinced than ever that Alaric's treasure is real."

"Alaric's treasure?" He looked to Maddock for a second, then back to Lina. "What treasure is that?"

Lina inclined her head toward one of the nearby exhibits.

"Come, let's walk." Maddock and Bones followed her into the museum proper. As they browsed the displays and took in the sights, Lina told the story.

"The basic story goes something like this. Alaric was the first king of the Visigoths. Prior to becoming king, he was involved in many conflicts, sometimes on the side of the Romans, sometimes in opposition to them. In the year 394 he led a Gothic force of over twenty thousand at the battle of Frigidus, where he and his men played a crucial role in assisting Theodosius, the Eastern Roman Emperor, defeat the Frankish usurper, Arbogast."

"Arbogast? Wasn't he a wizard in those Hobbit movies?" Bones asked.

Maddock frowned. "I thought you said Tolkien books and films are for geeks."

"They are. I just watch the movies so I can find new things to mess with you about."

Maddock rolled his eyes and turned his attention back to Lina.

"Please go on."

Lina grinned. "Alaric felt the emperor did not give him his due recognition for the role he played in the victory. He left the Roman army and was chosen as the "reiks" of the Visigoths, loosely translated as king. In the year 408, Emperor Flavius Honorius executed one of his most important generals and incited Romans to murder tens of thousands of the wives and children of Goths serving in the Roman military. This led the Gothic soldiers to defect to Alaric's army and prompted Alaric to march on Rome to avenge the Goth's murdered families."

"So he wasn't completely the bad guy in all this," Bones said.

Lina shrugged. "I suppose it all depends on perspective. History is often like that."

"What happened next?" Bones asked.

"They ravaged the countryside, and sacked several cities before laying siege to Rome. He eventually forced the Roman senate to free all forty thousand Gothic slaves in Rome. As was the norm at that time, alliances shifted, more conflicts broke out, and he besieged Rome again in 409 and in 410."

"That was when he finally broke through," Maddock said.

Lina nodded. "Allies within Rome open the gates for him and he and his forces spent three days sacking the city. By all accounts, they treated the population humanely, and only burned a few buildings. Churches were spared, along with the people who took refuge within their walls. They even refused to take privately owned treasures that Alaric felt had religious significance, and therefore 'belonged to Saint Peter.'"

Bones scratched his chin. "How did he and the treasure come to Consenza? If he was taking it home, he went in the wrong direction."

"He planned to conquer Corsica and then move on to invade Africa, but a storm destroyed most of his fleet. Before he and his remaining forces could head north, Alaric took ill and died here on the coast. Most researchers believe that his body, along with his horse and the fabulous hoard of treasure, was buried with the hoard inside a stone vault at the confluence of the Crati and Busento rivers – a spot which now lies in the heart of Cosenza. Up to eight meters below ground. The river was diverted while the vault was dug, then returned to its natural course. Afterward, the workers were executed in order to preserve the secret."

Lina paused to give her audience of two a chance to

ask questions, but Maddock and Bones both appeared to be in deep thought. "People have been searching for the treasure for years but have yet to find it."

At this Bones put on a frown. "Couldn't the treasure be at the bottom of the ocean where we found the shipwreck remains and the artifacts?" He nodded to the falcon and the dagger, still in her hands, but Lina shook her head.

"No. He wouldn't have carried the treasure along to Africa. It would have been a needless risk."

"That makes sense. So the treasure probably is still around here somewhere," Bones mused.

Lina cleared her throat, shifted uncomfortably. "I know this is not what you want to hear, but please, do not search for the Alaric treasure. I can't really explain, but things are difficult right now." She left it at that.

"You don't need to worry about us," Maddock said, choosing his words carefully.

She shook his hand and then Bones' before the two men left the museum.

CHAPTER 3

The *Ristorante Torquemada* had been recommended to Maddock and Bones by locals and so far the food did not disappoint. They decided to grab a real meal and come up with a game plan before heading back to their ship. They chose a table in the open air dining area, and now Maddock was halfway through his linguini with clams, and Bones his spaghetti, wisps of steam still streaming up from the hot plates. Maddock had tried to explain Bones that spaghetti was about as Italian as hot dogs and mustard, but Bones cared not a whit. The light chatter of other diners punctuated by the cooing of nearby pigeons was the ambient soundtrack as the two ate. After a while Bones narrowed his eyes and quickly turned his head back toward Maddock.

"Have these people never seen a red man before or what?"

Maddock looked casually about and then back to Bones. "Maybe just not such an ugly one."

"Screw you, Maddock."

They heard a chuckle nearby and turned to see a server who had clearly overheard them. Upon seeing they were watching him, he stepped over to their table. "Please forgive me, but it's just that, in Italy, we are very stylish." He cast a meaningful look at Bones' leather jacket and jeans.

Bones shrugged. "I make this look good. Besides, the chicks still like me. That's what matters, right?" Two girls at a nearby table giggled and he gave them a wink. The server's face creased in a disapproving frown, and he hastily departed. Bones then turned his attention back to Maddock, who was already back to swiping through articles on his smartphone.

"You learn anything new about this treasure?" Bones attacked another forkful of spaghetti while Maddock looked up from his phone.

"So far I've pretty much just corroborated what Lina told us." He tapped his screen, navigating to another page.

"Speaking of Lina, I noticed you chose your words carefully when she asked us not to look for the treasure." He flashed a knowing grin.

"I didn't lie. I told her she didn't need to worry about us, which is true. We can take care of ourselves."

"I'm glad to see I've rubbed off on you."

Maddock feigned an injured expression. "That hurts. Besides, I didn't say I wanted to actually search for the treasure. I'm just interested in learning more about it."

"Whatever." Bones frowned, his fork hovering over his plate. "There's something I want to know. After all this time, wouldn't the natural erosion caused by the river have uncovered the tomb by now?"

Maddock shook his head and explained. "Believe it or not, in the last 1,500 years the river bed has actually risen by about almost two meters, so his tomb could be up to eight meters below ground by now."

Doubt lingered in Bones' expression. "Do people take the legend seriously?"

"Yes, plenty of searches have been done."

"For example?" Bones dug back into his plate.

Maddock sipped from his glass of red wine before answering. "During the mid-18th century, a huge project took place to unearth the tomb of Alaric, but nothing was found. Then, in the early 19th century, writer and traveler Alexandre Dumas visited Cosenza after a major earthquake had drained the Busento River. Dumas reported that numerous people began fervently digging for the Roman treasure, but once again no treasure or tomb was unearthed."

Bones looked like he was choking down a mouthful of pasta in order to say something, but Maddock continued. "That's not all. In the 1900s, the accounts of the treasure attracted the attention of Adolf Hitler and Heinrich Himmler, who ordered an extensive search for the hidden loot. But they too came back empty handed." Now finished, Maddock speared a clam with his fork while Bones responded.

"I don't like our chances," he said simply.

Maddock thought about it for a bit. "What if they were all looking in the wrong place?"

Bones' eyes widened. He nodded to the women who had giggled earlier as they stood and left their table, then said to Maddock, "So then where should we look?"

Maddock exhaled heavily and dropped his fork onto his plate. "I don't actually know, and it might not be worth the trouble, considering all the red tape and treasure trove laws."

Bones took a swig of his Birra Moretti beer and said, "How much treasure do you really think we're talking about here?"

Maddock went back to his phone and scrolled down a web page, emitting a long, low whistle. "Up to twenty-five *tons* of gold—that's fifty thousand pounds—along with assorted silver and gems."

Bones raised his eyebrows. "I suppose that would be

worth the trouble."

"We told Lina we wouldn't look for it."

Bones was about to reply when two men walked up to their table. One wore a suit and tie while the other was dressed in a uniform. Maddock was pretty sure he knew what kind of uniform it was, but the badge that man presented removed all doubt.

"Gentlemen, we need to talk."

CHAPTER 4

"Cosenza *polizia"* was how the man in uniform introduced himself, in a clipped, no-nonsense tone. The other individual, wearing a trench coat and sporting a mustache, had a few more words. He reached a hand out to Maddock. "I apologize for interrupting your dinner, *signor*, but this is most urgent. I am Fabrizio Colombo from the *Ministero dei Beni e Delle Attività Culturali e del Turismo.*"

Bones raised an eyebrow. "The Ministry of Cultural Heritage Activities and Tourism?" He and Maddock exchanged looks. They both knew full well what this was about. *Cultural heritage* referred to artifacts, and more specifically to what they thought of as *treasure.* Neither said anything while waiting to see what Colombo had to say. They didn't have long to wait.

"May we speak outside?" Colombo asked.

Maddock looked ruefully at his half-full glass. "I haven't finished my wine yet."

Bones glanced around at the nearby tables. "And I'm still working on getting a few chicks' digits—that's phone numbers for you old guys."

The Italian men exchange frowns. Colombo said, "Again, gentlemen, I do apologize for interrupting your meal. By way of compensation, MiBACT will gladly cover your bill. Now kindly come this way, please.' The *polizia* cleared his throat while Colombo extended an arm toward the restaurant's nearest exit, directly off the outdoor dining area.

Maddock remembered what he'd heard about the Italian justice system—that it was corrupt and particularly tough on foreigners. He didn't know if that was particularly true or not, but that's what he had heard. Still, he nodded to Bones, and they got up from their table, Bones chugging down the last of his beer as the other three began walking toward the exit. Outside, they walked a short distance to the banks of the Busento River. It was small and shallow, hardly a river at all. Their conversation easily overcame the soft gurgling of its waters.

Colombo stopped near the water and addressed them seriously. "I understand the two of you are treasure hunters." It wasn't a question, but the implication was clear. Maddock responded without further prompting.

"Archeologists, actually," Maddock said. "Specifically, marine archaeologists."

The *polizia* stood a short distance away from the other three, keeping an unobtrusive yet sharp watch on their surroundings while Colombo continued to question Maddock and Bones. "So then I am mistaken to assume you are here for Alaric's Treasure?" He raised an eyebrow as if daring them to say he was mistaken.

Maddock shook his head after which Colombo gave him a long, hard look, but Maddock waited for him to speak first. Finally, the investigator grew impatient. "I understand you have, in your possession, *Signor* Maddock, artifacts that are rightfully the property of the Italian government."

Inwardly, Maddock cringed. This was even worse than he thought. He was hoping this was a cursory snooping around into possible treasure hunting activities, but the accusation made it crystal clear that their information was rock solid.

At this point, Bones interjected to say the artifacts were found in international waters. Colombo laughed in response. "Alaric's fleet was sunk in the Strait of Messina, which is far from international waters."

"That's crap," Bones said. "The wreckage we found wasn't in the Strait. It was further south, in the Ionian Sea. There are these things called currents, you see…"

But Colombo was having none of it. He instructed them yet again to turn over the artifacts. "I will take down your information, since in some cases a reward is paid to the finders of artifacts belonging to the Italian government." But the look in his eyes told them this will not likely be one of those cases. "We will accompany you to where you are staying in order to retrieve the artifacts."

Maddock didn't see what choice they had, so they walked back to the restaurant, where Colombo's unmarked car waited. Colombo got behind the wheel while the *polizia* rode shotgun and Maddock and Bones slid into the back seat. Maddock provided the name of their hotel and Colombo drove them there in short order.

Inside the room, Maddock allowed Colombo to follow him to the room safe, from which he pulled the dagger and one of the falcons and handed them to Colombo under the watchful eye of the *polizia*.

Colombo nodded but then asked, "What about the cross and the scarab?"

Maddock screwed up his face into a mask of what he hoped looked like genuine confusion. "Cross and what? I don't know what you're talking about. "He gestured to the open safe. "As you can clearly see, the safe is empty, but feel free to search our room if you like. Take your time. We've got all night." He folded his arms and waited for the detective to decide upon his next move.

Colombo nodded to the *polizia*, who then asked Maddock and Bones to accompany him outside. While the three of them waited just outside the closed door, Colombo proceeded to ransack the place. Maddock and Bones could hear drawers being pulled open, furniture being moved, objects being tossed around. After a few minutes, the door opened and Colombo beckoned them back inside.

"Gentlemen, thank you for your cooperation." The man sounded anything but grateful. "I encourage you to avoid any further artifact collecting without the proper permits. Otherwise, please enjoy your stay in Italy. It is my hope that it will not be necessary for me to pay you another visit."

Maddock and Bones bid their "guests" a curt goodbye and then closed the door to their room. They stood and looked around at their belongings strewn haphazardly about. Maddock appeared to be lost in thought.

"What are you thinking, Maddock?" Bones kicked an open duffel bag of his over toward the wall. Maddock took out his cell-phone.

"First, I'm going to call Willis and the crew and tell them to break off the dive and get the hell out of Dodge. Something tells me that just because we believe we're working in international waters doesn't mean the Italian officials will see it that way.

Bones nodded. "Definitely a good move. I'm sure those government assclowns would be more than happy to redraw the map just to do us dirty. What then?"

"As far as I'm concerned, Lina screwed us over pretty good. So, I no longer feel any guilt about possibly having misled her."

A grin spread across Bones' face. "That's what I'm talking about! Let's go find us some treasure."

CHAPTER 5

Maddock and Bones stood once again on the shores of the Busento River. They had made the short drive back here after steeling their resolve to find Alaric's lost treasure despite Colombo's warning. "Besides," Bones had said back in their hotel room, "who knows if those cop dudes will decide they forgot to look under a pillow or something and come back? Let's get out of here for a while." So presently they walked along the river bank. Shoulder high in some spots while only a couple of feet over the water in others, it showed signs of erosion and geological change over the years. After a while Maddock explained they were looking for a likely spot where the river could have easily been diverted.

Bones tilted his head to one side as he mulled this over. "That's assuming the earthquake back in the 1800s didn't change the river's course completely."

Maddock nodded in agreement as his right boot splashed into the shallow water, cool but not freezing cold, at river's edge. "We might need to find a local historian type we can trust. Someone who could fill us in on…"

Bones suddenly looked over his shoulder. "Speaking of locals…"

Maddock looked in the same direction to see Lina approaching on foot, looking abashed. "Gentlemen, I am so sorry. Please, can we talk? I want to explain."

"Hmm. Let me think. No." Bones turned and began walking in the opposite direction.

"Please. I owe you an apology. Just give me a moment of your time." Lina held her hands out in a pleading gesture. Maddock noted that her eyes said she was sincere.

Bones turned back around and started patting his pockets. "What do you know? Your apology isn't going to bring back the artifacts the cops took from us. Finds we worked hard for. Hell, one of our crew almost died recovering them."

Lina's face reddened but she doubled down. "May I remind you, Bones, that we both know those artifacts were *not* found in international waters."

"Funny, I don't recall you being there." Maddock took a step toward her. "In any case, that doesn't explain why you shafted us."

Lina took a deep breath and then shrugged. "You are right, I'm getting off track. The truth is fairly straightforward. I wanted the artifacts for the museum and I made a rash decision." She looked as if that was all she had to say, but then hurriedly added, "Besides, I would have made sure you received a handsome reward. That was my intention."

Maddock threw his hands up and raised his voice slightly. "Then why didn't you just ask us to make a deal?"

Lina's gaze traveled from Maddock to Bones and back before answering. "I didn't know if you could be trusted. How could I be sure? After all..." She let the statement hang in the air with the sound of the running river water.

Maddock put a hand out in the universal "stop" gesture. "I get it. Foreign treasure hunters possibly plundering artifacts from a wreck in Italian waters. I'm aware of the reputation some of our competitors have. But tell me this: will the artifacts we gave you be put on display at the museum?"

Lina shook her head. "Unfortunately, and this is not my doing, no. Colombo, he took them. He claimed the museum was too controversial. He also said there was no reason to believe the artifacts had ever been in Alaric's possession, and therefore had no connection to the museum." After a long pause during which neither man interrupted her, Lina continued. "I am afraid his attitude is all too typical. After some reflection, I've come to a conclusion. There is only one way to keep the museum open."

Maddock asked, "What's that?"

Lina smiled back at him. "We must find the treasure."

CHAPTER 6

Maddock and Bones had just finished unloading their equipment when they saw Lina waving as she trotted over to them. Maddock felt a rush of elation on seeing her holding up a piece of paper. She had come through with the permits. She had promised it would be no problem, and Maddock and Bones had acted accordingly, exhaustively preparing and transporting their treasure hunting gear. But as the hours wore on he had become concerned that maybe she was overconfident in her ability to obtain the permit in time.

Lina reached them, beaming as she looked down at the paper. "I told you we had nothing to worry about."

"Maddock still has that nasty infection to worry about, but penicillin ought to clear it up in a few weeks."

Lina and Maddock frowned at him and the museum curator went on. "Fortunately, I've been working on this application process for some time now, so it all fell into place."

"What about the museum?" Maddock asked. "I hope we aren't keeping you from your duties?" He nodded to the paperwork, but Lina shook her head.

"Everything is fine. My friend Bianca is minding the museum. Not that we get many visitors."

"Bianca…she sounds hot. Got a picture?" Bones asked.

Lina rolled her eyes. "I'll give you a clue. You know what your American actress Cathy Bates looks like?"

"Yes," Bones said slowly.

"Bianca looks like the man who played her son in that silly football movie."

"I can't tell if you're joking or not."

Lina laughed and rubbed her hands together." Let's get on with it, shall we? My permits are solid enough, but there's no need to attract undue attention. We should get in and get out as soon as possible."

Bones cracked a wide grin and started to let a joke fly, but Maddock cut him off by pointing out onto the river. "Although the river has been searched many times, those efforts, for the most part, literally scratched the surface."

Lina nodded in agreement and Maddock continued. "I've identified two places I think the river might have been most easily diverted, so we might as well start there, using the ground penetrating radar."

But Lina's brow was furrowed as she scanned the river from right to left. "I'm worried we might need to build cofferdams to block the water, which we probably won't be permitted to do. That kind of alteration goes above and beyond what we're currently permitted for."

Bones nodded. "It would be nice to have a dry workspace, but the thing is, fresh water is no problem. With saltwater it might be an issue, but this river is fresh water, so we ought to be okay."

Maddock looked away from the river to Lina and Bones. "Another factor is that soil conditions could limit how far the GPR will penetrate, but there's really nothing we can do about that."

Bones turned to Lina and said, "Maddock is always a ray of sunshine, isn't he?"

She smiled and said, "He's right, though. We had better get to work."

The three of them set up the ground penetrating radar unit, which looked to a casual observer like a high-tech lawn mower with an electronic display above the handlebars. After a round of diagnostics and testing to confirm the unit was operating as it should, Bones began wheeling the device over the area.

Lina studied the terrain as she paced alongside Bones with the machine. "Remember, we're looking for a large, rectangular object."

"Gee, thanks," Bones said. "I wasn't…" He bit off his sarcastic reply after Maddock shot him a look that said, *Don't piss her off, we need her on our side.*

Bones continued plying the area alongside the river with the GPR unit, making a U-turn when reaching the end of the likely zone to cover a track parallel to the way he had come. Bones paused a couple of times for an anomalous reading, but quickly ruled them out as false alarms, natural formations that triggered a radar signature that looked like it could be something manmade but wasn't.

As they worked, a small crowd of curious locals gathered near the shore of the river. One of them cracked a joke about there not being any lawn here to cut, which prompted Lina to explain they were conducting a "simple archaeological survey." The onlookers soon grew bored and moved on, and then Bones stopped pushing the GPR.

"Your turn mowing this thing, Maddock." Maddock switched places with Bones and got behind the GPR's handlebars. He proceeded to wheel the machine over the riverbank, searching for what might lie below.

CHAPTER 7

The sun was setting over the river, painting it in streaks of red, orange, and gold, when Bones reached the end of another GPR swath and took his hands off the machine, yawning. By now they'd already covered the two most likely areas, plus an additional one Maddock had identified during the GPR search. But still they had found nothing.

"It's not looking so good, is it?"

Lina sounded dejected, so Maddock tried to lift her spirits. "We've got plenty more space to cover. Don't give up yet."

Bones rolled his eyes in Lina's direction. "Typical Maddock. You should see him work a grid when we're out on the water towing a magnetometer. It's like freaking Mardi Gras to him."

Suddenly they were interrupted by three young men, one of them in a priest's collar. The newcomers looked down on the treasure hunters from the high river bank, and the priest, identified by Lina in a whispered voice as Father Romano, addressed them.

"Are you looking for Alaric's treasure here?"

"Good afternoon, Father. You cut right to the chase, don't you? Actually, we're just doing routine archaeological work on this site."

The priest and his two cohorts slid down the muddy river bank until they stood level with Maddock, Bones and Lina. Then he held out a hand to Lina. "I demand to see your permits."

Lina let out a bubbly laugh. "Father, with all due respect, that's hardly within your authority."

Romano raised his eyebrows at her. "Everything is under God's authority, is it not?"

Bones looked at Lina. "Unless this guy has a driver's license that says Yahweh, he can move along."

One of the men accompanying Romano said something to Bones in Italian. Neither Bones nor Maddock understood the words, but Lina blanched. Bones took a step closer to the visitors, smiling. As he stepped up to them, they realized what an imposing figure the Indian cut.

"I don't think you want my friend to translate that for me, *paisan.*"

The man who had spoken to Bones took a step back.

"You should not speak so to the Father. He is a great man."

"*Leccaculo,*" Lina said with a smirk.

"What does that mean?" Bones asked.

"You would say, kisser of bottoms?"

"Oh, a kissass. Nice one!"

Romano's face reddened and then he spoke. "The Pagan grave and its foul treasure should remain in the ground where it belongs." To underscore this statement, he spat on the dirt, and the two men accompanying him did the same from further away. "This undertaking is cursed, just as every other attempt to find this vile treasure has been."Then the priest turned and walked off, his associates falling into step with him.

"Friendly folks around here," Bones said, watching them depart.

Lina nodded. "Welcome to my world." Then she turned to Maddock. "What do you think we should do next?"

Maddock stared into the water of the river for a moment before replying. "I've got some thoughts, but would like to do a little more research first."

"We could go back to my office and strategize there," Lina suggested. Maddock and Bones agreed and the three of them began breaking down their gear.

At the museum, Lina led them to a back room where she said it would be safe to store the ground penetrating radar unit. As they left the storage room and began walking through the dark corridor to the main showcase area, Bones began to sense something was wrong. He wasn't sure what it was at first, but his instincts warned him that something was amiss. Sometimes he jokingly attributed feelings like this to his Native American heritage, but he supposed it was more a matter of having been in many tight spots during his life. He knew what a dangerous situation felt like. He glanced over at Maddock, who had his head on a swivel, clearly also recognizing that something wasn't right here. Lina was all business, though, walking purposefully ahead of them down the same corridor she had no doubt passed through countless times before.

They kept on until they reached the showroom, where Lina finally sensed her companions were acting strangely and turned around. "What is it?"

Bones pointed across the room to the far side. Lina followed his finger but couldn't make anything out. "What is it? I don't see anything."

Wordlessly, Bones looked about the space and then began walking across the floor to where he had pointed.

Maddock stayed where he was, watching his back, while Lina slowly trailed after him. Bones picked up his pace as he caught a glimpse of a young woman lying on the floor, her golden hair spilled out around her head like a halo.

"Body here!" he called out upon reaching the inert form. He knelt down and quickly picked up an arm and felt for a pulse. "Female; she has a pulse."

He heard Lina's feet pounding the floor as she ran to him. "Bianca! "she cried.

Bianca did not look like Adam Sandler. She was a slender, attractive woman with an olive complexion and long, honey blonde hair. Right now, though, he was more concerned with her physical state. He didn't see any obvious signs of injury.

"This is my friend I left in charge of the museum while I was out." Lina dropped to her knees beside them. She hugged her friend, asking her many times if she was all right. Meanwhile, Bones looked over at Maddock, who was making a slow, deliberate circuit of the room, keeping watch for unseen threats as he went.

Bianca let out a low groan.

"Easy, take it easy," Lina cooed.

"I feel awful."

"I don't see any obvious trauma," Bones said.

"I don't think I am injured." Bianca sat up a little straighter..

"What happened?" Lina asked.

Bianca blinked her eyes a couple of times and shook her head slowly. "I'm not sure. I don't know exactly what happened."

"Just tell us as much as you can." Bones said.

"Well, I didn't see anyone come in. But, I think I

remember someone grabbing me from behind and a hand with a cloth coming down over my face."

Bones and Maddock exchanged a glance. Bianca continued. "Someone must have slipped into the museum when my back was turned. I don't know what happened after I lost consciousness."

"*Porca miseria!*" Lina swore. "It means, 'Do pigs live in poverty,' she said in response to Bones' raised eyebrow, as she examined Bianca for injuries. "You would simply say, 'dammit.'"

"You people really are on a different level of swearing, here."

Lina stood and fished her cell-phone from a pocket.

"What are you doing?" Bianca asked, sitting up.

"Calling the *polizia*. We've had a break-in and you were incapacitated by the intruder. We need to…"

"There is no point."

Lina's finger froze, poised over the smartphone's call button. "Whatever do you mean, there's no point?"

Bianca took a deep breath. "I didn't actually see the person and there aren't any security cameras." She looked around the museum as if hoping to prove herself wrong.

"Cameras have been something I was hoping to add," Lina explained. "We do have some valuable artifacts, after all, not to mention our own personal safety—but it just hasn't been in the budget. That's going to change now, though, mark my words."

Maddock and Bones both nodded their approval, and then Lina went on. "I still think it's worth calling the *polizia*, though. I don't like the idea that some criminal can just walk in here and knock out my employees with no repercussions whatsoever."

"There's another reason." Bianca cut her off without making eye contact. She stared down at the floor while continuing. "I had a recent run-in with the *polizia*. I don't want to go into detail, but suffice it to say they consider me untrustworthy and I'd rather not deal with them since I'm fine." She finished by turning one of her arms back and forth while looking at it, as if confirming it was in fact okay. "Besides, the museum does not need any negative attention from the authorities, nor negative publicity."

Lina looked to Maddock and Bones, who both remained noncommittal. The treasure hunters knew that the less law enforcement involvement surrounding their operation, the better, but at the same time Lina and Bianca had to feel safe. After a deep breath, Lina said, "All right, but let me have a look at the rest of the place, see if anything's missing. Be right back, it'll just take a couple of minutes."

Maddock and Bones stayed with Bianca, assessing her condition a little more and helping her to her feet. By the time she had demonstrated she could walk okay, Lina returned.

"Someone has been in my files!"

Bianca started walking away from them. "Look, Lina, do what you have to do. Call the *polizia* if you have to. I'm going home." She continued walking toward the exit.

"Whoa, hold up," Bones said, trotting after her. "You sure you're okay to walk any kind of distance?"

"I am fine, really. I just need to get a little fresh air and walk it off."

They watched her until she reached the back door, Bones trailing slowly behind her, until she opened it and left. Then Maddock turned to Lina.

"Let me guess. Someone messed with the files relating to Alaric."

Lina nodded. "But the joke's on whoever took them, because I have everything scanned. I wonder if it was the priest?"

Bones, watching through the window next to the door Bianca had exited from, called out across the room. "I'm going to see if I can find out."

"What do you mean?" Lina called back.

"Your friend Bianca is lying." Bones slowly opened the door and slipped outside.

CHAPTER 8

The lack of streetlights on the narrow road worked in Bones' favor as he trailed Bianca. Sticking to the shadows was second nature to him, and he made use of his skills now as he kept hidden without losing sight of his quarry. As he stalked her, he reflected on how he knew she was being deceptive—the way her eyes moved when she explained her reasoning for not wanting the *polizia* to be called, for one thing, but more importantly, the lack of chemical smell back in the museum that would have indicated the use of chloroform. Bones had encountered it before and it left a telltale scent that he would not miss. And beyond all that was simply a gut feeling that said, *She's lying. Don't trust her before you check her out.* So he was doing it.

He watched her make a few turns, not stopping at a residence, but instead arriving at a nearby church. Bones hid in a cluster of thorny bushes while she opened the front door, a simple, unadorned wooden affair, and entered the place of worship. When she didn't return outside after a few minutes, Bones made his way to the front door, casually, so that if he was being observed he would look like a random churchgoer. Pulled the door open silently and slipped inside, instantly scanning the room.

He saw no immediate sign of Bianca, or of anyone, for that matter, so he walked quickly, though not in panicked fashion, to the nearest alcove and ducked inside. He was the only one there. No sooner had his eyes fully adjusted to the light than he heard the soft creak of a door opening.

He glanced across the large room and saw Bianca entering the confessional. He heard a few muffled words in Italian, and then she came back out, looked around. She said something Bones couldn't make out. A few seconds later the man she had been speaking to inside the confessional emerged.

Bones sucked in his breath sharply as he recognized who it was: Father Romano. The priest and Bianca embraced while kissing passionately. The display went on for entirely too long, but then again, Bones couldn't exactly blame the guy. He thought about what a lousy priest he, himself would make. No babes the rest of your life? Not going to work. And Bianca was easy on the eyes, too, he had to admit.

He watched as the two broke off their kiss and then Bianca drew a folder of some sort out of her shirt and handed it to the priest. He rifled through it, nodded, apparently satisfied. Then he snapped it shut and kissed her again. Bones strained to hear as the pair exchanged a few more words but he couldn't make them out from his hiding place. Then Bianca turned and walked to the rear exit of the church while Romano watched. After she left through the door, Romano followed her out the same way a minute or so later.

Bones waited for a couple of minutes to make sure the priest wasn't going to pop right back in. After a few minutes he slinked down the aisle to the same doorway Bianca and the priest had exited through.

He pressed an ear to the door to see what he might be able to hear, a conversation, perhaps, or maybe footsteps—anything that told him there were people who would see him as soon as he stepped from the building. But he could hear nothing. Bones stepped outside into the cool evening air and closed the door silently behind him.

And then suddenly he heard a voice—Romano's. The man couldn't be more than twenty feet away. Bones looked left toward the source and realized his good fortune. Romano was right around the corner of the church, meaning he couldn't see that someone was shadowing him. Bones considered ducking back inside, but the man's words kept him where he was. As the priest spoke into his cellular, Bones eavesdropped on the one-way conversation.

The priest had a rich, clear speaking voice that made it easier for Bones to eavesdrop on his end of the conversation. To whom Romano spoke, he didn't know, but he was doing his best to figure it out. It didn't help that the conversation wasn't in English. Bones recognized the language, though: German. In the SEALs, Bones had studied Spanish, because it seemed practical, and German because he hated the French. He wasn't conversant in the language, but he could still understand a bit. Enough to make out some of what the priest was saying…

"Looking for the tomb." Something about "Americans," followed shortly thereafter by, "In the river…" And then came a word that wasn't German at all— "Menorah."

"What the crap?" Bones whispered.

Finally, as the call ended, Romano spoke two words that froze Bones' marrow.

"I've got to get to Maddock, pronto," he said to himself, before turning and treading noiselessly the opposite way around the church.

CHAPTER 9

Alone in his and Bones' room at the inn, Maddock hunched over the tiny wooden desk while scribbling notes on a legal pad. A small laptop computer sat next to that, its web browser open to an assortment of sites he had been using to conduct research on Alaric's treasure. Many of the web pages were full of wacky conspiracy theories. He grinned, thinking of how Bones would really get a kick out of them. After a time Maddock, pushed the pad aside and rubbed his temples. The river, for all its promise, had thus far proven to be a dead end. He strained to think of a new angle somewhere in the mounds of the same information he'd already sifted through more times than he cared to remember.

Maddock stood and began pacing the tiny space while he reflected on what they knew about Alaric's burial. He ignored the confines of the dingy room he occupied and mentally transported himself to a rectangular vault, buried beneath the river, or allegedly buried there. Buried along with treasures taken from Rome, but surely not everything that had been looted. The Visigoth warriors would have expected their shares, and Alaric's brother, Athaulf, who took charge of the army, would have been foolish to give it all up. But even so, the grave goods alone would have tremendous value, both monetary and historical, and Maddock would love to find them if for no other reason than to stick it to the priest, Romano, and his cronies.

He reached the closet door again and whirled back

around, pausing this time instead of pacing past the beds to the front door. *But where to look?* The only people who had been privy to the burial secret were Athaulf and his workers, with whom the carefully guarded knowledge seems to have died. Maddock mulled this over for a while longer, and then an idea struck him, one powerful enough that he froze in place, arms frozen as if halted in mid-swing.

No sooner had the thought passed through his mind then the room door opened. The noise startled Maddock and he felt a spike of adrenaline as he realized he was just standing there frozen like an idiot while someone— possibly the *polizia* with the Ministry of Cultural Heritage official, or who knew…Romano and his henchmen?…barged inside the room.

But it was only Bones, casually ambling inside and swatting the door shut behind him. The grave look on his face did not make Maddock feel much better, however. He'd seen the expression before, and it never spelled good news.

"You all right Maddock? Looking a little jumpy. Maybe you should switched decaf."

Maddock relaxed his posture. "I'm fine. Just doing a little thinking about Alaric. You look like something's on your mind, though."

Bones nodded. He related what he had seen and heard by tailing Bianca on foot to the church, confirming that she was in league with the priest. Upon hearing this, Maddock tossed his head back and stared at the ceiling in frustration. He exhaled heavily.

"That's not even our biggest problem, though," Bones added.

Slowly, Maddock looked down from the ceiling and

leveled his gaze at Bones. "Great. So what is it?"

Bones made eye contact with Maddock for a moment before answering, as if to steel him for a response that he knew he would not find palatable. "Father Romano is working with some old friends of ours." He paused for effect and then added, "Heilig Herrschaft."

There was a long pause while Maddock's skin paled visibly at the mention of Heilig Herrschaft. "My favorite branch of The Dominion," Maddock said sarcastically.

"Mine too!" Bones' frown belied his words. He cracked his knuckles and looked around the room as if searching for something to punch.

Would-be spiritual heirs to the Nazis, as well as being Christian extremists in their own right, Heilig Herrschaft sought to cement their power through the discovery of religious artifacts that could prove the veracity of their claims or, in some cases, that held powers Herrschaft could harness. Maddock and Bones had encountered them more than once over the years, and the resulting mayhem was never heartwarming.

"I guess I shouldn't even be all that surprised," Maddock said at length. "The Visigoths were Germanic, so the tomb of Alaric has the potential to bolster Heilig Herrschaft's particular strain of nationalism. And let's not forget about the financial aspect."

"There might be a religious angle, too," Bones said. "The priest said something about the menorah. Of course, he doesn't know we already found that thing, and that it wasn't in Italy."

Maddock nodded, flashing on a remarkable find he and Bones had made years ago. He grabbed his legal pad and flipped through its rumpled pages. He came to a section he recognized and stabbed a finger down onto the paper with an audible snap. "One of the legends holds that Alaric made off with the menorah during the sack of Rome, and that it was buried with him. I didn't pay much attention because we already know what happened to it."

"Maybe there was more than one," Bones offered.

"Maybe," Maddock said. "Or maybe the menorah itself is only a clue." He flipped through more pages of his notebook until he tapped one of the pages again. His heart raced. Could it be?

"I think I've got it. I know where we're going to look next."

CHAPTER 10

Mendicino, Italy

The village of Mendicino lay only a few kilometers southwest of Cosenza. If not for the equipment they had to carry along, Maddock and Bones could have jogged there with no problem. Lina had taken the day off and, despite Bianca's duplicity, had once again asked her to watch the museum, without mentioning what Bones had seen. At first blush Maddock and Bones had seen the decision as foolhardy, but after grilling her about it they soon accepted the logic. It would arouse less suspicion if Bianca continued on as usual. In order to throw Father Romano off the trail, she had told Bianca that she, Maddock, and Bones were headed north to Quattromiglia to scan the confluence of two steams—the Emoli and the Sturdo. Hopefully, Romano and his cohorts would fall for the diversion and head off in the wrong direction.

Now, the treasure hunting trio wandered through a thin patch of forest in the foothills of the Santa Lucerna Mountains. The terrain wasn't difficult to navigate, consisting of hard packed soil with a light leaf litter covering. So far the trickiest obstacle they faced was the occasional raised tree root or errant rock. Bones casually lifted a foot over just such an obstruction and said, "Tell me again why we're going caving?"

"Two reasons," Maddock answered. "First, inside one of these caves is carved a rune that resembles a menorah."

"A thinly drawn one," Lina added.

"That brings me to the second reason. About forty years ago, a farmer came across a mass grave not far from here—twenty men, all with their heads cut off. Their bodies were dated by experts to approximately the time period of Alaric's burial."

Lina seemed to understand immediately. "So you think they were the men who dug Alaric's tomb?"

Maddock nodded enthusiastically as he ducked a low-hanging branch. "I do. I also learned that, according to a few different accounts, Alaric was buried 'along' or 'near' the river, not necessarily directly underneath it."

"But those same accounts are specific on the point that it's near the confluence of two rivers," Lina protested. Bones nodded as if that's what he were about to say, but Maddock responded.

"Put yourself in Athaulf's position. You can't erase every single detail of the burial unless you kill every man in your army, and that's not going to happen. So, you take additional steps to protect the truth."

"You tell a story that's almost true, but with some important details changed," Bones interjected.

"Exactly," Maddock said as they reached a small clearing in the forest where an obscure opening in a cleft of rock was barely visible. "It's time to get to work."

Maddock cursed under his breath as his flashlight grew noticeably dimmer. He shrugged off his backpack and dug out a fresh set of batteries, watching while Bones continued to scan the cave walls for any clue to the fate of the treasure. Maddock swapped out the batteries and shone his light anew on the cave's smooth and uninterrupted walls. He could see nothing significant and wouldn't let the others know it, but he felt like a sled dog near the end of the Iditarod race. All day long they'd been crawling through caves, tunnels and caverns. A few of the tunnels were so low they had to scoot along on their bellies. The cavern they now found themselves in was one of the larger ones they'd encountered so far.

"I'm not seeing anything in here, Maddock," Bones called out, breaking him from his exhausted stupor.

"Me neither," Maddock returned.

"Nor I," Lina chimed in from her position on the opposite cavern wall from Bones.

"Let's head topside, then" Maddock said. The three of them made their way to the cavern's exit and then followed a narrow, upward sloping chute until they came out above ground in the clearing where they had started their hunt. There were multiple passages leading underground in the area, though most of them were not easy to find. But the one they now emerged from was not the same one where they had started out. The clearing was the same, but not the cave entrance. As the sun began to set, the trio looked around the clearing some more, checking for passages underground they might have missed. After a few minutes, Lina stopped walking and put her hands on her hips.

"Maybe we should call it a day?"

Maddock looked around while nodding slowly. "Sounds good. I think…" He broke off in mid-sentence as his gaze lingered on something. He focused on it for a few seconds, recognizing it as a narrow, partially concealed fissure.

"What is it?" Lina asked, following his gaze but not seeing anything noteworthy.

"On second thought," Maddock said," maybe we should give it one more try."

Lina's expression betrayed her disappointment. She held up her banged up elbows and pointed to her ripped jeans through which bruised knees were visible. "I'm not going to lie. I'm getting pretty tired of abusing my body to no end."

"She's right," Bones said. "I can think of much more rewarding ways to abuse one's body than that."

She cursed him in Italian and Bones grinned in response. "Relax. Why don't you take a break? I'll check out that opening real quick and see if it's even worth descending into."

Lina agreed to that and she and Maddock remained where they were while Bones jogged over to the newly sighted fissure. He disappeared behind a clump of foliage but a few minutes later they heard him call out. "You two owe me a beer. This looks good!"

CHAPTER 11

"**The sun goes** down pretty soon, Maddock. We gotta make this fast," Bones said. Lina agreed as she aimed the beam of her light up ahead of Maddock in the narrow cave tunnel.

"It's not like it's going to get any darker down here," Maddock said, looking around the narrow, pitch-black cave. "This passage is so narrow I don't see how it could go on for very far. Let's just check around this corner up here and then we'll head back."

Bones grunted in agreement as Maddock angled his body in order to wedge it into the fissure that jogged off to their right. Working his way into a new corridor, Maddock was surprised to find himself in a long, narrow tunnel with passages leading off left and right at various intervals. A narrow, web-like arrangement of fissures and cracks, he knew that they now had a dizzying array of options for which way to go.

And that was when an anomaly on the right-hand wall caught his attention. A crude drawing that Maddock recognized as being a rune, part of the Germanic alphabet. Playing his light over the stunning find, Maddock could see that it was shaped almost but not exactly like a menorah. An odd-looking base, with the seven candles seeming to hover over it. Oddly, only one of the candles is depicted as lit—the second from the right.

Bones and then Lina reached Maddock and they added their lights to the menorah drawing. Lina, her interest renewed, checked her watch. "It's definitely going to be night time if we don't head back soon, but, like you said Maddock, it won't get any darker in here and I think it's worth a little night hike after we get back topside to see what this is all about."

Maddock nodded. He used his smartphone to take a flash picture of the rune, and then said, "Let's move into this passage." They begin to explore, working their way deeper into the base of the mountain. They moved relatively easily down the tight straightaway, but Maddock paused when he reached the first of several new passages that branched off to the right and left. "Let's check this one out."

He ventured into the right-side passage, which was even narrower than the main tunnel. Each of the cavers had to turn sideways to be able to fit between the cave walls, but it was passable and before long Maddock came to a dead end. The group had no choice but to turn around and file out the way they had come until they reached the main passage again.

"Geez that only took like an hour," Lina said, her patience clearly growing shorter.

Maddock ventured further into the main passage until he reached another offshoot, also on the right side. "This one opens into a decent sized cave, Maddock noted. But he continued down the line, Bones and Lina trailing behind him, playing their lights around the passage walls. Up ahead Maddock shone his beam down another open cave mouth, but again, he opted not to explore the side passage in favor of walking down the main tunnel to see what was happening with the branching passages.

He reached another passageway, this one on the left

side, that led somewhere. He passed it and proceeded down the tunnel until the next right-hand passage, stopping there while he waited for Bones and Lina to catch up, shining his light on another cave on the right side just before the main passage came to a cul-de-sac.

Lina heaved a heavy sigh on reaching him. "Lots of possible cave offshoots in here. And to think we were looking mostly at the right-hand ones. I guess we'll have to investigate every one of these passageways, plus any on the left side of the main passage."

"In detail," Bones agrees. "That's how Maddock likes it."

"Maybe not," Maddock said, his gaze focused on the picture of the rune on his phone. Then he trained his flashlight back down the main passageway from the way they had come. "I've got an idea."

CHAPTER 12

Bones looked around the cave as if assessing its vastness before leveling his gaze at Maddock. "Care to share your idea with us now, or is it something that can wait until I'm belly up to the local watering hole back in town?"

Maddock shook his head. "This definitely isn't something we'd want to discuss in a bar. And it's easiest to explain here, while we're looking at it."

"Looking at what?" Lina asked.

"You remember the rune on the cave wall that looks like a menorah?" Bones and Lina nodded and Maddock went on. "I think it may not be just a simple rune, but that it serves as a map."

He gave them time to digest this while he pulled his phone from his pocket and brought up the picture he'd snapped of the rune. He pointed to different parts of the image as he addressed them. "Look here: The main passageway is the center of the rune. The side passage we just followed had three caves branching off, just like the three arms of the menorah. I'll bet the other passage also has three branches."

Bones' eyes grew wide with understanding. "And the candle that's lit marks the way!" He clapped Maddock on the shoulder. "You know, Maddock, you're a genius, unless you're wrong, that is, in which case you're a dumbass."

"It won't take too long to find out." Maddock pointed down the passage. "Let's head back the way we came, this time checking the openings on the other side of the cave; that's the right side as we head toward the main exit."

The three explorers crept cautiously through the tunnel, watching for the right-hand passages. As predicted there were three branches. When they reached the third, confirming the accuracy of the menorah depiction, Maddock led them back to the second opening. "This one's the next to last, the one that matches the lit candle on the rune. Let's see if it leads somewhere interesting."

Maddock felt a surge of hope right away as he peered into the new route with the aid of his flashlight. Much wider and easier to navigate than the others they explored, it extended straight back before gently curving into the darkness. "Plenty of room for once," he remarked.

"This way would be the easiest I've seen yet to carry loads of treasure," Bones said hopefully.

"Or a body," Lina added sourly.

They walked into the cave, almost a cavern it was so spacious. Other than negotiating a slight downward incline, it was smooth walking. Which meant it didn't take long for them to reach the back of the cave after it curved, at which point they realized it was another dead end.

"End of the line," Maddock declared. All of them looked around, stabbing their beams into the dark recesses of the cave, hoping to see something besides bare, natural rock.

Bones let loose a few choice curse words while Lina leaned against a boulder to rest, taking on that exhausted look again. But Maddock was lost in thought, staring at the cave ceiling, shining his light around. After a bit it fell on an odd formation- a rounded stone, like an inverted bowl, with seven stalagmites propping it up. He pointed to it.

"Tell me what you see there."

The museum curator's jaw dropped. "It looks like a menorah."

"That's not what I see," Bones said.

"Well, not exactly like a Menorah, it's upside-down, but still..." Lina backtracked, but Bones waved away her clarification.

"You know what I see?" Maddock said. "I see seven stalagmites in a cave that has no other stalagmites or stalactites."

"You're right," Bones said. "Holy crap."

Lina giggled.

"What?" Bones asked.

"You say 'holy crap.' In Italy, we say *cavalo*."

"Why is that funny?"

"It translates to 'cabbage.'" She turned away from Bones' puzzled expression and looked up at the stalagmites. "You believe these are fake?"

Bones looked to Maddock. "Only one way to find out."

It took some doing, but with some careful climbing atop the nearest boulders, Maddock and Bones were able to come within arm's reach of the mysterious rock formation that hung from the cave ceiling. Upon reaching it they pulled, pushed and prodded the strange bowl every which way, to no avail.

"It sure *feels* like normal rock," Bones said, pulling his sore arms back down to his sides. "Maybe we should call it a night, go for a beer, and come back in the morning with some blasting equipment." Lina nodded with gusto before Bones continued. "And I mean a pitcher of beer in a frosted glass, I'm too tired to twist the top off of anything."

Maddock's eyes took on a faraway look. "*Twist the top...*" He stared up at the incongruous rock formation, seemingly in a trance. "I think that's it."

Bones and Lina now stared up at the rock bowl, then back down at the arrangement of stalagmites jutting up from the cave floor. "Everybody grab one!" Bones ran to the nearest stalagmite and put both hands around it. Lina and Maddock did the same, Maddock positioning himself on the pinnacle of rock opposite Bones.

"Righty tighty, lefty loosey," Bones quipped. The three of them heaved, attempting to spin the entire formation counterclockwise. Nothing. They tried again, and this time something broke free with an audible pop. There was a rush of dry air as the entire structure pivoted to one side, revealing a short drop into a new chamber below.

The look on Lina's face was priceless. She jumped up, ran to Maddock and gave him a massive bear hug, which he returned awkwardly while looking at a snickering Bones over his shoulder.

"Hey, what gives?" Bones asked. "We all know I'm the genius here."

Lina finally released Maddock and he said, "Well, maybe not a genius, but you do find more nuts than the average blind squirrel."

Lina looked a little confused at the expression, but she didn't care. She proceeded to drop down into the chamber after the most cursory shine of her light.

"Lina, no!" Maddock shouted. But his warning came too late. As Lina landed in the sub-floor chamber, its floor shattered with series of sharp cracks.

CHAPTER 13

Lina clung to a jagged slice of floor that still remained, crying out and swinging her legs into open space below. Maddock mentally kicked himself for not keeping a closer eye on her. Clearly she was not used to this type of work. She was accustomed to studying artifacts brought back to her from places such as this, not to being part of locating and retrieving them.

"False floor!" Maddock yelled down to her.

She surprised him with her response. "Yes, I managed to discover that on my own."

At least she's a little more collected than I gave her credit for, Maddock thought.

"Heads up!" Maddock turned in the direction of Bones' voice in time to see a rope flying his way. He caught it and immediately unraveled it enough to drop one end down to Lina, who let out a curse.

"Cazzo! My phone, it fell!"

"Never mind that right now. Grab the rope."

Lina's hand swiped out and clawed the rope to her body just as the remaining sliver of floor gave way.

"Brace yourself!" Maddock heard Bones cry out. He dropped to the floor, legs out in front of him, heels digging into the cave floor against Lina's sudden weight free-falling at the other end of the rope. Bones moved swiftly to wrap the slack rope around one of the stalagmites., winding it around until it would support the stress.

"Got it, you can let go."

Maddock did so, tentatively at first—moving his hands just off the rope to see if it would hold. After seeing it didn't budge, he stood and walked to the edge of the new opening. "Lina?"

"I'm okay!" her voice echoed up. "I've got the rope. And I think I can see the ground. I'm going to lower myself down."

"Lina, wait for us!" Maddock sprang into action, tying a new line around another of the stalagmites and then dropping down into the pit. Bones followed suit from another stalagmite, lest they should put too much weight on a single one. Together Maddock and Bones descended right through the shattered false floor, not bothering to stop and test their weight on what little remained of it. As they slid steadily down the ropes, they caught sight of a faint glow far below—Lina's fallen cell phone.

Maddock paused as he neared the end of his rope, which still dangled in mid-air. But he could see the ground wasn't that far below his feet, it was just that it sloped sharply. The flashlight had landed here but then rolled down to more level ground somewhere out of sight below, where only the weak part of its spreading beam could be seen.

He looked over at Lina, dangling a few feet away from the stalagmite Bones had tied her off to, and Bones, some distance away from her. "I'll go first, then you, Bones. Lina, you go last so we can help break your fall if need be. The drop isn't far but landing on a slope is tricky. You have to be ready to roll as soon as you hit. Ready?"

Maddock counted down from three and let go of the rope. He landed facing sideways to the slope—right leg further down the hill than his left. He lost his balance and went down but was able to dig a heel into the dirt—the ground was still dirt, his mind somehow registered—stopping himself from rolling all the way down. All the way down to what, he didn't know, so as soon as he regained his footing he shone his light down the incline. He saw only that it leveled out onto a spacious passage that led out of sight.

"I see a big passageway down here. Bones, come on down. I'm out of the way."

As soon as he finished his sentence he heard the dull thud of his friend's feet hitting the uneven subterranean ground. Bones began to roll downhill but Maddock reached out an arm and halted Bones' downward progress.

"It's all downhill from here. Right, Maddock?" Bones grinned as he dusted off his pant legs.

"Let's hope so. Come on."

Lina dropped down last, and immediately retrieved her phone, which she declared dead. "You will have to call my land line if you need me."

With bigger priorities than a phone on the men's minds, they moved along the passageway down into the depths. Maddock led the way with Bones and Lina right behind him. When they reached the bottom, Lina picked up her fallen flashlight and the three of them moved into the darkness ahead. The passageway was a natural one, but up ahead was something clearly constructed by humans. Maddock was the first to reach it but Bones was first to comment.

"A freaking door! No way!" A stone door with an iron ring in the face was set into what would otherwise be the end of the long passageway.

The three of them examined the surfaces all around it, above and below, but could detect no signs of a trap.

"Could it really be this easy?" Bones asked. "Behind this door is the vault?"

Maddock shrugged. "There's only one way to find out." He and Bones both put a hand on the large ring and pulled.

He hadn't expected that his first attempt would be successful. Surely there was some hidden locking mechanism they'd have to overcome. But, to his surprise, he felt it give. Slowly, with a grating rumble, the door swung outward.

Maddock shone his light inside and his heart raced as the beam of his light fell upon a stylized eagle, a popular symbol among the Visigoths, carved on the far wall. But his moment of excitement dissolved into disappointment as he looked around.

"Now we know why it was so easy." The lackluster tone of Bones' voice registered his disappointment even more than his words. "It's a vault, all right. But it's empty."

They stepped inside and Maddock encouraged them to take a look around the empty chamber anyway, but as expected, they found nothing. No treasure, no clues, no hidden passages or trapdoors. There was nothing here. It was a dead end.

"I can't believe we went through all of that trouble only to get down here and find an empty room," Lina said.

"I had a bad feeling when I saw the door was unlocked," Bones said.

Maddock leaned up against one of the walls while he mulled over their options. "What do you think happened here? This space is obviously a vault." He looked around at the low chamber comprised of tons of solid rock, deep beneath the ground. At the stout door set into the base of it.

"Do you think somebody got here first?" Bones asked. "Cleaned the place out?"

Lina shook her head. "Things like that don't remain a secret. In modern times, antiquities like this appear on the black market. If it happened centuries ago, it would have become part of local legend. But there's never been so much as a whisper."

"Let's think about the treasure itself," Maddock said. "If Athaulf took the treasure, it's safe to say he probably divided it among the Visigoths."

Bones threw up his hands and gesticulated to the empty room. "Why would they bother to build a vault if they weren't going to hide any treasure in it?"

Lina looked around thoughtfully before answering. "I think maybe they did hide it here. They couldn't take the treasure along on their planned invasion of Sicily and North Africa, so they built this vault for safekeeping. Then, when the fleet sank and Alaric died, they divided the treasure and moved on."

"And the clue with the menorah?" Bones asked.

Maddock thought he knew. "They needed to keep the treasure hidden until they returned for it, but they were going to war. They couldn't risk the secret keepers dying, so they left behind a clue that could lead those in the know back to this place."

Bones grimaced. "This sucks."

Maddock raised a finger in the air. "There is one bright spot to all this. It proves the legend is true and that Alaric's grave is out there somewhere. We just have to find it."

CHAPTER 14

Cosenza

"**Do you mean** to tell me that you have never had gelato?" Lina asked. She and Maddock strolled along the narrow sidewalk, taking in the sights of Cosenza. Bones had joined them at first, but had quickly spotted a pair of attractive young women enjoying food and wine in the outdoor dining area of a local *osteria*. In typical Bones fashion, he had pulled up a chair and the party of two quickly became three. Maddock and Lina had gone one without him. He doubted he'd see his friend for several hours.

They passed a trattoria, and Maddock inhaled deeply of the delicious aromas that wafted out onto the street.

"I've never had genuine Italian gelato." He rubbed his stomach. "I have to say, if I lived in Italy I'd probably be at least twenty pounds heavier than I am now. The food here is amazing."

Lina flashed a sly smile. "I'm sure some lucky lady would see to it that you got plenty of exercise."

"In that case I might have to start looking into real estate," he kidded. Before he could follow up with a flirtatious comment, Lina seized his hand.

"Here! The best gelato in Consenza."

She led him into a small, brightly lit gelateria with polished floors, crisp white walls, and a bright green ceiling. Lina ordered *nocciola* for both of them, assuring him it was the best. They found seats outside and sat down to enjoy their desserts.

Maddock found the gelato to be richer and denser than ice cream. The *nocciola* proved to be a delicious blend of hazelnut and chocolate.

"This is incredible," he admitted. "I'm not usually a dessert person, but I think I could handle seconds."

Lina explained that gelato was made from the same custard base as ice cream, but had a higher milk content, and less cream and eggs than its counterpart.

"It is also churned at a much slower rate," she explained, "which makes the gelato denser than ice cream." She paused, looked deep into his eyes. "But you should not have a second serving."

"No? Why not?"

"A full stomach is no good for…other nighttime activities." The wink she flashed him left no doubt what she meant.'

"You know, after such a rich dessert, I think a long walk is in order."

"I agree. My *appartemento* is not far. Perhaps you'd like to escort me home?"

"I'd be delighted to." Maddock hoped he'd be invited in.

Just then, a dark-clad figure approached them. Maddock turned to see an elderly woman clad in a nun's habit. She addressed them in Italian. Lina's eyes went wide, and she replied sharply. The nun leaned in and whispered something into Lina's ear. Before Lina could reply, she stood, turned to Maddock, said, *"Uomo bruciato,"* then disappeared into the darkness.

"I hesitate to ask, but what does uomo bruciato mean?" If it translated to "keep your pants on" he was going to be sorely disappointed.

"Burnt man," Lina said, frowning.

"Was she talking about me? I've got a pretty good tan going, but no sunburn."

Lina laughed and shook her head. "She was delivering a warning. She said we should not search for the treasure or else the burnt man might harm us."

"The burn man," Maddock said slowly. "What is he? Some sort of local ghost? Some sort of bogeyman who guards Alaric's treasure?"

"I have never heard of such a legend. Let me see." Lina took out her phone and grimaced. "I forgot I need to replace this." She held it up so Maddock could see the shattered screen.

"I got it." Maddock took out his own phone and searched burnt man legend Italy. "Let's see what we've got. *Burning man concert.* No good. *Italian man burns girlfriend to death when she refuses oral sex.* Sounds like a real charmer. *Giordano Bruno.*"

Lina shook her head. "No good. He was a philosopher who was burned at the stake for heresy."

Maddock made a few more searches, looking for ghosts or legends that might have a connection to a burnt man, but turned up nothing.

"I think it's safe to say there's no legend," he finally concluded. "Maybe our friend the priest has an ugly friend who's after us?"

Lina shrugged. "If that is the case, then I definitely want you to walk me home. Shall we go?"

It was a short walk back to her apartment and when they reached the front door, Lina didn't put the key in the lock. Instead, she turned and thanked Maddock for a lovely evening.

"You're very welcome," he said, a touch disappointed that she apparently was not going to invite him inside.

Lina bit her lip. "You know, Bones is probably back in your room with at least one of those two women. I would hate for you to walk all the way back only to find a *Do Not Disturb* sign on the door."

"It wouldn't be the first time," Maddock said.

"Why should he be the only one to have fun?"

Before Maddock could come up with a clever reply, Lina's arms encircled her neck. He felt her body, soft and supple, pressed against his. Their lips came together in a deep, passionate kiss.

Eat your heart out, Bones.

CHAPTER 15

Bones was asleep when Maddock returned to their room. He opened one eye, glanced at the clock, and sat up straight. "No freaking way! You and Lina?"

"No comment," Maddock said.

"So you didn't hook up with her? Let me guess, you sat around playing bridge and talking about your feelings."

"As a matter of fact, we did hook up." He felt his cheeks burn as Bones let out a hearty laugh.

"It's too easy with you, Maddock. But way to go. She's hot."

Maddock didn't reply. He sat down and began removing his shoes.

"Dude, don't tell me you feel guilty."

"No, it's just not appropriate. We're colleagues."

"Right. Colleagues." Bones flopped back down on the bed.

"So, how was your night?"

"Good, not great. We had fun, but it turns out they're sisters and they had this crazy idea that their friendship was more important than one of them getting to know me better."

"You gotta hate that," Maddock said with a laugh. "Oh, by the way, we got a weird warning from a nun." He filled Bones in on the burnt man. His friend agreed it was weird, but felt it was far too late at night to try and figure it out. Maddock couldn't disagree. Exhausted, he undressed and was asleep almost as soon as his head hit the pillow.

What seemed like only seconds later, he realized with a start that his smartphone was ringing. Groggily, a confused dream involving Lina wearing a nun's habit still fresh in his mind, he snatched up the phone from the nightstand beside the bed and accepted the call. Before he say hello, a familiar voice rang out.

"Maddock, it's Lina. Are you there?"

The urgency in her voiced snapped him awake. "Yeah. Sorry, I'm half asleep. What's wrong?" He looked at the time on the phone. It was one o'clock in the morning. Something must be wrong.

She lowered her voice to just above a whisper. "There's someone outside my *appartamento*. I'm not sure who it is, but he seems suspicious. He's just skulking about."

"He hasn't tried to break in or anything?"

"No. I don't suppose I can say for certain that it's my home he's interested in, but he keeps looking this way, then looking around. I called the *polizia* but no one has arrived. The person on the other end of the line reminded me that it was not against the law to walk down the street at night."

"We'll be right over. Just stay put and stay on the line."

Bones was awake now, and had inferred from Maddock's side of the conversation what was happening. He sprang out of bed and hastily dressed.

"What do I do if he does try to get in and no one is here?"

Maddock had managed to dress while talking on the phone, and now he and Bones rushed out into the hallway, headed for their rental car.

"One option is to see where he tries to enter. If he tries to come in through the front, you can go out the back, or vice-versa. The other option is you go into a closet or bathroom and secure the door handle to something solid using a coat hanger or something like that.

"All right." Lina took a long, deep breath. "It's probably nothing. I've just been anxious lately. Probably letting my imagination run wild. I'm sorry if I'm wasting your time."

"It's not a problem. We'll be there soon."

The roads were nearly deserted this time of night and they made good time, with Maddock driving above the posted speed limits but not recklessly so. They didn't need any more encounters with local law enforcement. As he drove, he kept Lina updated on their progress by speakerphone.

They were only a few blocks from Lina's place when she let out a gasp.

"He's not there."

"The man who's been watching your place? Maybe he left." At least, that was what Maddock hoped was the case.

"But he disappeared so suddenly. I only turned away for a moment and then…"

They heard a cacophony through the phone speaker—a crash followed by a single scream.

"Lina!" Maddock and Bones shouted. No reply. And then the call ended.

Maddock floored it and the car accelerated with a screech of rubber. Bones pointed out Lina's building up ahead on the left, and Maddock pulled the car up to the curb a few doors down. Bones was out of the vehicle before it had come to a complete stop, in time to see a compact Fiat streaking out of sight, the lights blinking off just before it made a right turn onto a road that led out of the residential neighborhood.

Bones made a move like he was ready to jump back in the car and chase after them, but Maddock waved him away. "I'll follow them. You go inside and check on Lina. Maybe she's hurt." He turned and looked in the direction of Lina's home and saw the door begin to open. Instinctively he cut the engine, turned out the headlights, and told Bones to get back inside the car. The latter was unnecessary. His friend had recognized the situation and quietly slid his bulk back into the small car.

A man emerged from the first-floor apartment. Maddock recognized him as one of the priest's underlings. He lit a cigarette and gazed in the direction the Fiat had gone. After a few seconds he slowly turned and looked in the direction where Maddock and Bones were parked. The two slid down until they could barely see over the dashboard, an easier task for Maddock than it was for Bones.

"When he turns around again, I'll go after him," Bones said quietly. "I'm sure he knows what's up with Lina." He paused. "What if she was in the Fiat? We'll need to know where they're taking her."

Just then, three more men emerged from the apartment. The last closed the door behind him.

"They don't look like much," Bones said. "I think we can take them."

"If even one of them is armed, we're screwed," Maddock said. Besides, these guys look like grunts, heavies. Who's to say they know anything?"

"So what do we do, then? Follow them and hope they

take us to Lina? Assuming someone has taken her."

"Small town, empty roads, I don't think we could follow them without being noticed."

"And if they know they're being followed, they definitely won't lead us where we want to go." Resignation hung heavy in Bones' voice.

"I've got an idea. We'll lay a trap for them." Maddock punched up Lina's number and then they watched as the men turned and went back inside. The answering machine picked up.

Maddock shot Bones a knowing glance before saying into the phone, "Hey Lina, sorry to call in the middle of the night, but I've just found something you'll want to hear about. I've made a *major* breakthrough. Listen, do your permits cover the cave system outside of Mendicino? Specifically the southernmost, the one closest to the river? I'm sure hoping they do. As soon as you get this message, give me a call no matter what time it is. We need to get on this right away, before anyone else finds out. Call me."

Maddock ended the call and waited. Seconds later, the men returned to the street. Excitement shone on their faces as they hurried away. As soon as they disappeared around a corner, Maddock and Bones dashed to Lina's apartment. It took only a few seconds to confirm their fears. Lina was gone.

"What's the plan?" Bones said.

"You up for a run?"

CHAPTER 16

Mendicino

Back inside the same cave they only recently left, Maddock and Bones made their way a short distance past the entrance and then stopped. They had left their rental car behind and run the short distance to the caves, not wanting the attention a vehicle might draw, and crept unseen to the cave.

Heads on a swivel, they watched and listened for any signs of human activity. Detecting none, Bones knelt and examined the cave floor where it joined the right side wall.

But he wasn't looking for treasure this time. "I think this'll work for the first trap. It's one of my personal favorites. Keep an eye out while I get to work."

Maddock agreed and Bones set about his task. The trap he had in mind was one he had learned as part of his Native American heritage. A simple design with formidable, though not lethal effects, Bones had already collected the raw materials he needed in the woods outside the cave. He unclipped a folding metal shovel from his small pack and used it to dig a wide hole a couple of feet deep. About halfway down the hole, Bones inserted a circular array of sharpened sticks into the dirt such that they held fast and were angled slightly downward.

Maddock peered into the hole with interest while Bones explained his handiwork.

"Good old Apache foot trap. The foot goes in, but it

doesn't come out. Not without a struggle, anyway. This won't kill anybody, though. Worst it could do is break an ankle."

Maddock nodded. "It'll slow these guys down, and that's what we need."

"Apache," Bones said with a grin.'

"If you say 'jump on it,' so help me…"

"You ruin everything," Bones said as he selected a few of the leafy boughs from the pile he'd gathered outside the cave. "Watch and learn, Maddock. This would go faster if we both set the traps after this one."

Maddock observed how Bones disguised the opening of the foot trap with leafy branches. Maddock noted that this close to the entrance, seeing leaf litter inside the cave wouldn't be unusual, but that deeper inside it might actually attract attention.

Bones agreed. "Let's just say that the foot trap isn't the only one I know. I still think we can use the foot trap again, though. I did notice places where rains have washed debris further into the cave. But I'll mix it up so they don't get too comfortable with any one thing."

"Sounds like a plan. I'll make another one of these further in."

"I'll work a different section of the cave and meet you back at the vault chamber in…" Bones checked his watch. "Fifteen minutes."

Maddock also consulted his timepiece before nodding. "Let's not try to lead them right to the vault if we can help it. We need to see them enter, and we need them not to get lost on the way there. How about at the beginning of the menorah passage—ahead of the drawing?"

Bones agreed. "Makes sense. Okay, so see you in

fifteen."

"Don't take a minute longer than that. Those guys are probably on the way right now."

The two operators split up and set about constructing traps in different parts of the cave system. Fifteen minutes later, they converged at the designated spot near the menorah.

"All good," Bones reported, slightly out of breath.

"Same here, I set two more foot traps."

Bones nodded. "So now we wait."

Maddock held up a hand for silence. As soon as Bones stopped talking, they heard a shout of surprise and a pained outcry, followed by hushed chatter.

"Sounds like they found the first of my foot traps," Bones said, face expressionless.

More voices, soft but still carrying well throughout the subterranean system. Maddock pointed further down the corridor, away from the direction of the footsteps, and he and Bones soft-footed their way there.

Hiding behind a small outcropping of rock with their flashlights off, they had one foot trap between them and the intruders. Without knowing how many men had invaded the cave, however, it was a small measure of comfort. Maddock picked out at least three distinct voices as he crouched behind the jutting rock. Any thoughts he had of the men retreating after one of them fell prey to the booby-trap were quickly dispelled as the sounds of heavy footfalls grew louder by the second.

Bones put a hand on Maddock's shoulder and held up three fingers. "Foot trap number two in three….two…one…."

Another cry of pain echoed off the tunnel walls.

"And we have a winner!" Bones finished.

"Let's go!" Maddock sprung up and ran deeper into the main menorah passage, bypassing the right-hand tunnels until he was in front of the left-side one that led to the vault. He took one side of the passage, while Bones took up a low-profile position on the other. Looking back, they saw three men pursuing them down the passage, running fast and with much anger.

As the trio of marauders was almost to Maddock and Bones' hiding spot, Maddock could see they were armed—each man carried a at least a gun in hand, a sheathed knife on a belt, and one man carried an automatic rifle slung over his back. He knew he and Bones would need to be extremely careful. Though he doubted Bones could have missed it, he made sure his friend knew the newcomers were armed by pointed to one of the weapons. Bones nodded in return, his eyes taking on that familiar look Maddock had seen so many times before—a look the Indian got when mentally prepping for a battle in which they were outnumbered and outgunned.

The flashlight beams of the intruders swept closer to Maddock and Bones' positions. The men reached the side passage in front of them and paused to shine their lights down its open chasm. For whatever reason, they decided their quarry was not down that way and continued down the more inviting main passage, taking them right to Maddock and Bones.

Bones made the first move. His swiftness was disarming in and of itself, but the strength of his muscles combine with a practiced coordination took care of the rest. The man nearest to him made the mistake of turning his back to Bones, who promptly lashed out with a leg behind the man's calf while simultaneously pulling him backward. He landed on his back on the cave floor, Bones extending him the courtesy of placing his foot on the exact spot where the back of the man's skull was about to crash into the ground one second before it happened.

That didn't stop him from stomping a boot down on his victim's solar plexus, though. He needed him to stay down but didn't want to cause him any lasting damage if that was left on the table as an option. He had some fleeting recognition of this man as being one of the priest's henchmen who had paid them the little courtesy visit down at the river site. Yet he had no time to dwell on this fact, since one of the man's compatriots now swung at him with a full-fledged haymaker. Bones ducked the right arm in a blur, catching Maddock out of the corner of his eye side-stepping a punch thrown by one of the other two assailants. Could the reason they hadn't opened fire yet be that they wanted the treasure hunters to lead them to the exact X-marks the spot location of Alaric's hoard?

Bones reached up and grabbed his assailant's wrist after the punch missed, and pulled it down and twisted, sending the man sprawling while snapping the wrist with an audible *pop*. Bones watched him writhing in pain on the ground and, satisfied it wasn't for show, he moved to the man. Quickly he knelt and frisked him, checking for weapons. He found a snub-nosed .38 and a folding knife, and relieved the man of them.

He heard the scuffling of feet increase in intensity behind him and whirled around in time to see Maddock enter into what looked like a boxer's clinch with the fighter. Both men had their fists pressed into the other's and continued to circle around. Maddock went for a quick headbutt but missed, and then his opponent tried the exact same thing, almost missing completely but grazing his left ear.

Bones sprung over and gave the man a solid kidney punch, dropping him where he stood. Again he went through the motions of patting him down, and again he did not come up empty. He handed Maddock a 9mm Luger and showed him a Leatherman Multitool, which among other things, featured a 3-inch knife blade. Maddock pointed away from them at that moment, at a fourth man fleeing away from them toward the cave exit.

"Let's go!" Bones pocketed the multitool and ran down the main passage with Maddock toward the fleeing interloper. The corridor was a long one, and the two ex-SEALS passed the many side-passages in a blur. Their target moved at a considerably slower pace, not because he didn't know he was being chased, but because he simply wasn't that fast, and was completely unfamiliar with the layout of the cave to boot. Maddock got to him a half step ahead of Bones and launched himself onto the man just has his prey turned around to see how close his pursuers were getting.

Maddock used his foe's body as a shield as they hit the ground. He heard his quarry grunt heavily with the impact, and then, as Maddock had counted on, Bones was also on him in a flash, securing his arms at his sides.

"I got him, you can get up," Bones told Maddock, who promptly released his grip on the adversary and stood back a step. He looked around briefly, checking for additional men lurking in the shadows, but saw no one and so turned back to the man, whose face was being jammed into the dirt by one of Bones' boots.

"Ease up, let me get a look at this fine specimen of

humanity," Maddock said. Bones stepped off the guy's head, and the tackled one looked up at Maddock, who promptly flushed red.

"Romano!" Bones blurted out, unable to contain his surprise.

"Well, aren't we the lucky ones? Looks like the head honcho decided to make a personal appearance." Maddock looked angrier than Bones could ever remember seeing him. "I would have thought he would bring Lina as a guide." He shook his head while contemplating her situation. No such luck. She could be anywhere now. He lifted Romano from the ground roughly and shook him by the collar of the leather jacket he wore over his cassock.

"Where is she?"

"If you ever want to see her again, you will let me go now."

Maddock took on a stern expression. "That's not how it works, Romano. You see, my friend the Indian, here, has this thing for…let's call it *persuasion*. He's always got these nifty tricks up his sleeve to help him persuade people. What have you got for us tonight, Bones?"

Bones took off his backpack and opened it. "Let's see…I think I've got a bottle of petrol, a piece of string, and two sharp sticks. Right here…" He stuck an arm deeper into his pack.

"Okay, okay. I'll tell you what I know," Romano spat. He glared up at Maddock before turning his gaze back to Bones, watching his backpack carefully while Bones stared at him, awaiting his response.

"She's in the dungeon beneath the castle."

Bones laughed out loud, a bellowing chortle that

bounced around the cave walls, making it seem even bigger than it was. "Stop telling fairy tales, the castle is a tourist attraction."

To Bones' surprise, Romano nodded. "That's true. The dungeon entrance was sealed off years ago, but few people know you can get to it through the sewers. They use it as their headquarters."

Maddock narrowed his eyes at Romano. "Who's 'they'?" he asked, but he already knew the answer, which Romano confirmed.

"Heilig Herrschaft."

Bones aimed a confused glance at Maddock. "I don't get it. Why would an Italian priest hook up with radical German nationalists?"

Even in the dim artificial light of the cave, the touch of defiance was visible on Romano's face. "I am descended from Athaulf himself. Visigoth blood runs in my veins, and the treasure is rightly mine."

"So, what's the deal?" Maddock asked. You get the treasure, and they get the menorah?"

Romano paled. "How did you…how could you possibly know that?"

"You wouldn't believe me if I told you." Maddock signaled Bones and together they bound Romano's wrists and pulled him to his feet. "Let's go, holy man."

The priest nodded, even smiled at them as he faced toward the distant cave exit. But the smile disappeared when Maddock and Bones forcefully whirled him around and began marching him back through the menorah passage they had just traversed.

"Hey, what's going on now! You promised to let me go if I told you what you wanted to know! We're going the wrong way!"

"We will, if you've told us the truth. But we're going to leave you here for safekeeping while we verify that. If you've lied to us, Bones will come back with his petrol and sharpened sticks."

Romano gasped. "What? I told you the truth. I'm not worried about that. But what if you don't make it back for some reason, any reason?"

"If we don't make it," Maddock said, "at least you'll be able to enjoy the treasure vault that is rightly yours."

They reached the end of the passage where the vault entrance was and turned into it. Romano gasped.

"You…you found the treasure?"

"Not the treasure," Maddock clarified, "just the vault." He pushed Romano inside and closed the door.

Then Maddock turned to Bones. "What were you going to do with the gas and the sticks, anyway?"

Bones grinned and shook his head. "I have no idea."

CHAPTER 17

The Castello Normanno Svevo di Cosenza occupied a grassy plateau atop Pancrazio Hill, a sizable rise that was not so tall as to justify calling it a mountain. Maddock had done his research on the landmark back at the inn, and now, as he and Bones walked up the footpath leading to its main entrance, he mentally reviewed what he had learned.

The Saracens, a group of European Christian writers, had built the castle in the tenth century, and since then it had been through many additions, remodels and retrofits. One of these was a pair of octagonal towers, one of which was still present and visible to Maddock now as he squinted up at the castle.

Its role over the centuries varied considerably, from serving as home to Emperor Frederick II and his son Henry VII, to Louis III, to use as a prison in the 1500s and 1600s. Earthquakes damaged the castle sometime during this period, rendering the structure unfit for use. A century later, however, new additions were made by Archbishop Capece Galeota, who transformed the property into a seminary. During the 1800s the castle was used as a fort as well as a prison again, and once again, earthquakes did more damage.

To Maddock it was a miracle the place was still standing at all.

"We going in or do you just want to stand here and admire the architectural beauty of it all?" Bones prodded. Maddock looked up at the stone walls—some of them in good shape and with tile roofs on top, while others were mere crumbling facades of their former selves.

"We're going in, Bones, but we can't just waltz in through the main gate like everybody else." By "everybody else," Maddock meant the single family of three that was strolling along the main walkway, ahead of them, about to enter the castle's front gate. The place was open to tourists, but traffic was pretty light.

"Ah, the sewer system, right?"

Maddock nodded. "Where else? Seriously, it leads to the dungeon, which is in the basement section of the castle, off-limits to the public."

"So we've got to tunnel in like rats."

"Now you're getting it. Come on, let's look around for the entrance. Try not to make it too obvious." Maddock proceeded to stray a bit from the manicured path. His research had informed him that there should be a sewer entrance that looks sort of like a capped well, with a metal cover of some sort. Expecting it may very well be overgrown, he eyed the vegetation carefully. A mixture of tall grasses and slightly overgrown hedges bordered the main walkway and extended out from there. Bones began to look around also, his unwavering gaze probing the foliage for any anomaly that might indicate the presence of an entrance.

Maddock continued his way along the path, rooting into clumps of bushes here and there while Bones ventured farther afield, well away from the beaten path. Maddock grew concerned.

"You'll attract attention before long out there."

Bones put a finger to his lips. "I hear something."

Maddock said nothing while he waited for Bones to figure out what it was. The Indian turned his head slightly in either direction, then fixated on a spot. "Running water. Hold on, this is worth the risk to check out."

Maddock paralleled him from the path as Bones walked toward the castle, but out in the untended foliage. After a few meters he crouched and looked around again, then low crawled through some shrubs until he called out barely loud enough for Maddock to hear. "Got something."

Maddock looked casually around to see if anyone was observing them, but if they were, he couldn't tell. He strayed from the walkway and moved quickly to Bones' location in the middle of untamed plant growth. His friend was shoving aside an unruly collection of brambles while duck-walking a step at a time deeper inside what was clearly an opening into the ground.

"It goes through to something," Bones said swiping more thickets out of his way.

"Right behind you." Maddock took one last 360-degree glance around, and seeing nothing, followed Bones into the earth. The dank smell of wet soil permeated the air as the two ex-warriors followed a downward gradient. The sound of flowing water grew louder as they made their way deeper into the opening; Maddock thought of it as a culvert.

"This must be it," he told Bones, who flicked on his flashlight and illuminated the space they now found themselves in. The running water was not deep. Bones stepped through it without getting his ankles wet, although the stream did take up the entire culvert, sort of like a drain pipe. Ahead, the conduit stretched out of sight at a slight downward incline.

The pair of former SEALs followed the wet tunnel

for perhaps a hundred yards, until they came to a fork. One of the branches went down sharply, almost like a waterfall, while the other continued straight ahead. Maddock surveyed them both for a few seconds before giving his thoughts. "This one that stays flat looks like it heads back to the castle ground floor.

"Restroom overflow?" Bones surmised.

"While this one," Maddock continued after making a face, "definitely looks like it could lead to the dungeon. It goes deeper, that much is for sure."

Bones walked right up to the edge and shone his light over the drop, emitting a low whistle. "That's a nice little plunge, I'd say fifty feet."

Maddock caught up to him and leaned out also. "It's not vertical. Let's go." He sat on the edge of the precipice and then pushed off with his hands, sliding down the watery drop. Bones followed suit and Maddock knew it must have taken all of his restraint not to let out a whooping holler. The need for silence on a mission had been instilled into him during his time in the SEALs, though, and so he made the exhilarating slide in complete silence, the big grin on his face the only indication he was having fun.

They hit the bottom hard enough to not be able to stay on their feet, but not so hard as to sustain any injuries. Rank water flowed through the passage, and a bevy of rats scurried away from the cone of light as Maddock directed his flashlight down the sewer.

"Stinks to high heaven in here."

"I've smelled worse," Bones said. "One time in Tijuana I met this chick…"

"I get the picture. Let's move out."

The pair picked their way down the sewer, seeking

out occasional dry spots as stepping stones while avoiding the rats, some as large as footballs. "I don't see any trash down here," Bones observed. "No cans or broken bottles or anything. When I was a kid this would have made the perfect hangout."

"Could be a sign we're on the right track if no one ever comes down here. I see some kind of wall up ahead." They were now deep into the sewer and without flashlights it would be pitch black. They came to the wall Maddock had seen—it was made of stone with a metal grating set vertically into it, from which water flowed out. The spacing between the metal bars was far too small for a person to fit through. Maddock tested the bars by pulling on them. Although they wouldn't budge, he noted they were rusted and weak.

"Maybe we could take some kind of tool to it," Maddock suggested.

"I've got just the thing." Bones shrugged out of his pack and rummaged inside it while Maddock provided light. After a few seconds Bones produced an average sized claw hammer.

"Seriously?" Maddock asked. "You walk around with a hammer in your pack?"

"I said I have just the thing. Not kidding. It's a little heavy for every day carry, but you'd be surprised at the jams it gets me out of."

Maddock shook his head. "Not surprised at all, actually. Go ahead. Hopefully it gets us out of this one."

Bones stepped up to the grate and swung the hammer at one of its bars, which cracked on the first hit. He repeated the process on several neighboring bars and then Maddock kicked them out of the way with his boot. It would still be a tight fit, but there was now room for a man to squeeze through if he was careful about it. "I'll go first," Bones said. "If I can make it, we know it won't be a problem for a little guy like you."

Maddock shook his head at Bones' jab. "I'm six feet, Bones. Little guy? Really?"

Bones grinned as he passed through the twisted metal cage easily. He chuckled to himself as he stalked off into the darkness, flashlight illuminating a sewer that was wider but with a lower ceiling than the one on the other side of the grate. They walked straight for a few minutes until a waterfall cascaded from above. They paused in front of it.

"What do you know?" Bones said, "A literal waterfall of crap!"

Maddock shone his light beam through the curtain of falling sewage. "I think there's something back there.

Bones, who had been gazing upward at where the sewage came down from, now followed Maddock's light. "I hope so, because we're not getting up there, even with ropes."

"I don't think we'll have to. I hope this sewage is pre-treated, though, because we will have to get wet."

Bones groaned. "It really is Tijuana all over again. What are we dropping into?"

Maddock studied what he could see through the curtain of foul-smelling liquid. "Not sure. Looks like a solid floor about ten feet below, though."

"Good enough for me. Wait, did you say *floor*? As opposed to *ground*?"

Maddock shrugged. "It looks pretty smooth. I can't really say for sure."

"Only one way to find out." Bones leaped through the waterfall.

And then Maddock thought he heard something. He called down to Bones in a voice he hoped was loud enough to overcome the falling water but not so loud as to be heard by whoever it was he heard talking. "Turn off your light."

Maddock looked behind him to see if anyone was approaching from the same way they had, but things were still in that direction. He looked back down the drop to see Bone's swatch of light go dark. "Move left, Bones. I'm jumping right." Maddock took the plunge, slipping through the falling stream on the right side, hoping Bones had heard him so that he didn't land on his friend.

His feet impacted the wet floor—it was a floor, he couldn't help but think in a flash—safely away from Bones, who crouched a few feet back in the darkness. As soon as he situated himself, Maddock saw that Bones was pointing straight ahead into the distance. Where the voices were a little louder.

The two crept closer, one hugging each wall. In here a channel was dug into the floor where the sewage ran, leaving a narrow but dry aisle on either side. Aside from not having to trudge through sewage, this meant they could move more quietly, avoiding the splash of water. The voices grew louder and soon Maddock could make out two men talking. Shortly after that, he could see them. Neither wore a uniform of any kind, but both carried automatic weapons along with holstered pistols. Whatever it was they were guarding, Maddock thought, it must be serious.

They still weren't quite close enough to make out the words of the conversation, but soon one of the men nodded to the other, turned around and left. He walked deeper into the underground complex, which widened to a roughly square shape where the guards were keeping watch.

Maddock motioned to Bones to move ahead. The Indian acknowledged the signal with a nod, the resolve in his eyes not visible in the darkness. For the first few steps the guard still faced away from them, watching his associate leave the room into a side passage or hallway until he was out of sight. But when they were a mere twenty feet or so from the guard, he suddenly wheeled around on a heel.

Maddock and Bones froze in place, well aware that the guard carried a flashlight on his utility belt. He didn't use it, though, only stared into the darkness for a couple of seconds and then turned back around. Maddock saw his hand disappear into his pocket and he tensed, wondering if the guard had in fact spotted them and was now pulling out a gun after pretending like he hadn't seen anything. But the glow of a smartphone materialized instead.

And then a new worry for Maddock: was he calling for backup, or to report suspicious activity down here? Yet the guard also carried a walkie-talkie on his belt. And then he saw the man tapping away on his phone screen, swiping through web pages like so many relaxed workers during a spot of downtime. No, Maddock thought, he's not alert to our presence, he's only surfing the web.

That was when Maddock noticed the guard's earpiece, the coiled wire leading from it to the radio clipped to his belt. They would have to be very careful. He might have a lip mic, too; it was too dark to tell from this distance. Maddock began moving again, very slowly, silently, toward the room the man guarded. He saw

Bones doing the same on the opposite side of the sewer, wraith-like in his movements.

The guard never really had a chance. The pair of ex-SEALs converged on the man while he paced lazily away from them. Maddock went high and Bones came in low; the guard was laid out flat and unconscious in four seconds, without so much as a gasp. Bones relived him of his weapons, tucking the pistol into his own waistband as a backup, but tossing the automatic into the sewer. Maddock, meantime, took the headset and radio, hoping to catch some intel that would help them find out what exactly they were up against.

Then he signaled to Bones they should move deeper into the complex, and the two moved out in the direction where the fallen guard's associate had gone. Hallways stretched out both to the left and straight ahead, but it was what lay to their right that immediately captured their attention. A spacious room ringed by barred cells. Occupying the main space were medieval instruments of torture that appeared far too new to be original.

On one of the devices, Lina was stretched out on a metal rack. Above her hands was poised a wicked-looking blade. It was all Maddock and Bones could do not to rush to her aid on sight, but standing over her was a powerfully-built, hideously scarred man. Maddock and Bones recognized him immediately. "Issachar," Maddock whispered.

Maddock felt Bones tensing, about to spring. Maddock eyeballed their trajectory to the disfigured captor. Satisfied he had picked out the course that afforded him with the greatest likelihood of success, he planted his back foot to spring off of.

And that was when Issachar looked right at them. He smiled and said, "My old friends! Welcome."

CHAPTER 18

Suddenly Maddock heard footsteps on the stone floor. Two armed men stepped out behind them, and another man in front of them. Maddock and Bones were ordered to raise their hands in the air, and they both did so without hesitation. They knew when they were outgunned. The men, most likely they were guards who had been keeping better watch than he had given them credit for, ordered him and Bones to move into the torture device room. The command was in Italian, but they got the gist of it anyway and proceeded to march toward Issachar and the machine to which Lina was strapped.

"Stop. That's close enough." Issachar's voice echoed slightly in the chamber, but the hand he held out in front of him was unwavering. Maddock wasn't sure that his own hands, still held in the air, were that steady. He couldn't believe his eyes. For there was Issachar, an agent of the Dominion whom he had now twice believed dead, standing before him. How was it even possible? His face was badly scarred, and one of his arms ended in a hook where his hand ought to be. So this was the burnt man.

"It's been a long time," Issachar began. "How's Jade Ihara doing?"

"Moved along," Maddock said, his voice flat. "I guess I wasn't enough man for her."

Issachar laughed threw his head back and laughed. "Of that, I have no doubt."

But Maddock and Bones knew not to try to make a

move with all of the guards around. "It's strange," Issachar said when he was looking at his two newly arrived captives again, "I almost think of you as a friend. We've been through some amazing things together, haven't we?"

"Speaking of that," Bones cut in, "How did you get out from under that mountain, anyway?"

Issachar's expression grew more intense. "That wasn't easy. "They had their fun with me before they grew complacent." He held up his left hand, which ended in a stump and a hook. "I do miss my hand, I'm not going to lie, but this can be fun too." He moved back a couple of steps and then ran the hook along Lina's cheek until he curled it around her throat. He looked up at Maddock and Bones, leaving the hook in place. "I have other implements at my disposal, too, but I really enjoy the classics."

"What the hell are you doing here?" Bones asked. "Seriously."

Issachar stared down at Lina's hook-snared neck while he replied. "Just trying to get ahead in the game, like anybody else. Working myself back into Heilig Herrschaft's good graces. Using my toys here…" He made a sweeping gesture with his remaining hand that took in the torture devices, "…to prise information from the locals."

Maddock appeared incredulous. "And no one else has found out?"

Issachar cackled lightly, causing the hook to jostle slightly on Kina's throat. "It's the old-timers who have the best information. I extract what knowledge I can before they expire, and then we drop them off in their beds. Romano does a masterful job of comforting the family, if there is any, and generally smooths things over."

Maddock shook his head in disgust, telling himself to move on before his emotions got the better of him. "So what are you after? You , of all people, know the menorah isn't here."

Issachar nodded with a huge smile, as though he were about to laugh. "And behold, a lampstand all of gold with its bowl on the top of it, and its seven lamps on it with seven spouts belonging to each of the lamps which are on the top of it."

Bones nodded. "You're quoting Revelation."

A look of surprise registered on Maddock's face, and Bones explained. "Forced to go to church camp every summer as a kid." Bones then turned to Issachar. "If I remember my scripture correctly, that quote is symbolic and refers to the seven main churches of the time."

Maddock mentally pictured the strange rune, and then it clicked for him. "You're after a *literal* bowl. One of the seven that inflict misery on the followers of the Beast of Revelation."

Issachar nodded. "They'll come in handy when Heilig Herrschaft comes to power, don't you think? I'd prefer the one that causes earthquakes and hailstorms, but even the one that inflicts foul and malignant sores will do nicely in a pinch."

"And you think Alaric possessed it?"

"I'm investigating any and all legends associated with a menorah. I like to be thorough."

Maddock shook his head slowly. "You always were a sick bastard, Issachar."

The villain shrugged. "I get the job done. Speaking of which, the two of you doubtless have some information I will find useful." He nodded to the closest of his guards.

"String them up."

CHAPTER 19

Neither Maddock nor Bones had any desire to see if they'd be able to get out of whatever predicament awaited them on Issachar's torture equipment. Together the two ex-SEALs moved as one.

Maddock whirled, grabbing the man guarding him and spinning him about. He ducked as the man in front of them opened fire, the bullets smacking into his comrade, held in Maddock's vice-like grip. At the same time, Bones grabbed the man guarding him, controlling his gun hand, and drove him backward like a lineman setting a block.

The man on Bones had only an instant to realize what was happening before Bones drove him back into the spiky iron maiden. He let out a shriek of sheer pain and terror before the door slammed on him.

Maddock took the dead man's fallen gun and rolled to the side as Issachar's last remaining gunman fired his final bullet. The round sliced across Maddock's thigh and he rolled into a crouching position. He squeezed off two rounds, taking the man down with a wheezy gasp.

Bones was a blurry specter flashing past him as he gave chase to Issachar, who fled through a doorway on the rooms' far end. Maddock was about to go with Bones, but Lina's panicked voice cut through his nervous system.

"Help me!" To Maddock's horror, Issachar had set the blade swinging, and now it glided only inches above her bound wrists.

Just as Bones reached the main exit to the torture chamber, a spiked gate slammed down, very nearly impaling him. Bones tried to raise it, muscles straining until he thought he would rupture something, but to no avail.

"Forget the gate, Bones! Help me stop this thing!" Maddock eyed the monster blade as it swung like a scythe, ever nearer to Lina's pale exposed flesh. Then he whirled around, looking for anything that might help him shut off the deadly mechanism. He spotted two unlabeled levers, but had no idea which one to pull.

"Maddock!" Lina screamed. "Do something, please! Anything!"

Stomach lurching, Maddock reached for the lever on the left, hoping it was the right one, meaning that it somehow shut off the swinging blade. His fingers touched it, but before he could pull it, a metallic crunch sounded from behind him. He turned around to see that Bones had jammed a suit of armor between Lina and the blade, which embedded itself deeply into the metal over Lina's trussed body. She exhaled heavily with the impact, and no doubt it didn't feel good, but it spared her the blade.

"Nice one, Bones." Maddock moved to Lina and together, he and Bones cut the museum curator free and helped her out of the rack.

Bones looked around the room, at the bodies of the dead guards strewn about on the floor. "What about Issachar?"

Maddock also briefly surveyed the grim space. "He's probably gone, but we'd better keep on the lookout just in case."

After taking a few minutes to collect some of the

fallen men's guns, they tried the lever Maddock had been about to pull to try and stop Lina's blade. The gate that had nearly impaled Bones rumbled open. Maddock looked over at the dented suit of armor that had saved Lina's life and shook his head. "Let's go."

The three of them left the grisly scene behind, trekking into the sewer.

EPILOGUE

Busento River

The roar of earth moving machines and heavy equipment operating in the riverbed below was like music to Maddock's ears. Bones and Lina stood next to him as they watched the veritable hive of activity below while workers went about excavating the riverbed. Up on the bank, the trio wasn't alone.

Colombo was here, too. Once they'd reported Lina's kidnapping and Romano had been arrested, there had been no way to hide their search from the government, and so had reached out to Colombo for help. The Cultural Heritage official had legally arranged the state-sponsored excavation based on the information Maddock and his team had provided. Under Maddock's guidance, they had found the site of the mass grave, then drawn a straight line from the cave and to the river. Sure enough, ground penetrating radar scans revealed a rectangular object buried beneath the earth.

Now, they all stood eagerly watching and awaiting the results. After some chit-chat about various technical details on the excavation process, a worker called up to the state official from below. "Sir, we're ready to open the vault!" Colombo turned to Maddock, Bones and Lina.

"Look, we wouldn't be in this position if it weren't for you three. You're welcome to come down there with me and have a look."

The four of them made their way down the bank of the river to the bed and walked over to a crane that now lifted a heavy lid that looked to Maddock like it was made of stone. When the massive piece was swung safely out of the way, the four of them peered down into the tomb. It was still dusty from the excavation, and Lina covered her mouth with the top of her shirt. But as their eyes adjusted to the scant, dust-filtered light inside the vault, they were able to pick out a pile of skeletal remains, as well as numerous ancient weapons—blades, clubs, shields—along with what was clearly the skeleton of an animal. Bones pointed out that one set of bones wasn't human.

Lina uncovered her mouth to reply, her voice low and tinged with excitement. "I think it might be a horse." She turned to Colombo. "Can we get a closer look? Can we go inside?"

He nodded and then motioned to his workers that they were coming through. The four of them entered the vault by dropping about six feet down to a surprisingly smooth floor constructed of interlocking stones.

"It is a horse!" Lina said upon closer inspection of the pile of bones. "And I know whose."

"Let me guess." Maddock stood over the human skeleton. "Alaric's."

Lina and Colombo both nodded. "The bones will have to be DNA tested," Colombo said, nodding to the human skeleton. "But I think it safe to conclude we have at last come across the remains and final resting place of Alaric I, leader of the Visigoths."

Maddock nodded as he walked up to a very old-looking wooden chest which had rotted partially apart, spilling some of its contents. "And his treasure." Gold coins, bars and a rainbow of glittering jewels littered the bottom of the tomb around the chest, and there were many more chests like it scattered around the vault. Still, Maddock's eyes continued to search until he spotted what he was looking for.

He had been looking too high, expecting what he sought to be placed on some kind of pedestal or altar, but when he finally laid eyes on it, the object of his search was at ground level. Resting simply on the tomb floor in a far corner was a golden bowl and seven golden lamps. The rest of them followed his gaze.

"Do you think they're real?" Bones asked.

Maddock knew better than to pick up the artifact in order to see if it was as heavy as gold should be. Especially with a museum curator and a Cultural Heritage minister in his presence. He knew each item would be obsessively cataloged and treated according to state-of-the-art preservation practices. Still, it was all he could do not to pick the thing up.

"I don't know, but it doesn't really matter. As long as Heilig Herrschaft thinks they are, they won't be safe in Cosenza."

"For once, I don't think you'll need to worry about that." Lina indicated two men standing nearby, dressed in uniforms Maddock didn't recognize as being part of any Italian law enforcement organization.

"They're from the Vatican."

"Enough said. We're in good hands." This from Bones.

Colombo stepped away from giving orders to a group of workers to shake hands and congratulate Maddock, Bones and Lina. "Once again, excellent job." He directed his gaze to Maddock. "Please also extend my thanks to the rest of your team aboard your ship." Maddock said he would and Colombo went on. "Again,

I'm sorry we got off on the wrong foot, but…" He waved a hand at the scene inside the tomb. "…these matters are sometimes complicated."

Then he turned to Lina. "You know, *Signorina* Franco, I think at this point that the Alaric Museum has a most promising future indeed, including a major increase in no-strings-attached funding. The government will be proud to support your operation from this point forward."

Lina brought a hand to her mouth in surprise. At length she said, "I don't know what to say. Thank you. I…"

Colombo held up a hand. "It is I who should be thanking you, Signorina Franco, for your careful stewardship of many of our country's most important heritage items. But that brings me to the following point." He made extended eye contact with her to show he was serious. She waited for him to continue.

"If you are going to display Alaric's tomb and grave goods, we will need to make sure your premises are highly secure."

Lina beamed, her elation temporarily overcoming her ability to speak. Colombo smiled at her and then turned to Maddock and Bones. "I am most certain a reward will be coming your way as well. Strictly monetary, mind you," he said sweeping an arm at the treasures stacked around the tomb. "The artifacts themselves must remain in the custody of Italy. But suffice to say I think you will be able to fund additional treasure hunts for years to come."

Both Maddock and Bones thanked Colombo sincerely, after which the cultural affairs official excused himself and returned to supervising his site workers.

Maddock turned to Bones, a satisfied grin on his face. "Great job. Ready to head back to the boat, rejoin the crew? Long voyage home."

Bones tilted his head, as if in thought. "I guess so, but you know, I really wish I had some more time to hook up with some of these local chicks."

A female voice behind them said, "Speaking of that…" Bones and Maddock turned around in time to see Lina grab Bones, pull him toward her and kiss him deeply. Maddock shook his head, laughing softly while he walked away.

"Some things never change."

The End

About the Authors

David Wood is the USA Today bestselling author of the Dane Maddock Adventures and many other titles. Under his David Debord pen name he is the author of The Absent Gods fantasy series. When not writing, he co-hosts the Authorcast podcast. He and his family live in Santa Fe, New Mexico. Visit him online at www.davidwoodweb.com.

Rick Chesler holds a Bachelor of Science in marine biology and can often be found diving, boating or traveling to research his next thriller idea. A former contractor for the U.S. Dept. of Commerce and the State of Hawaii, he currently lives in South Florida with his family, at the edge of the Bermuda Triangle. Visit him online at rickchesler.com.

Made in the USA
Coppell, TX
26 December 2020

47146409R00080